PACT

Philosophy. Politics. Religion. God's Plan

Oscar Pulido Fuentes

CONTENTS

"I want to thank you for choosing this educational book. PACT's objective is to broaden your knowledge, help you analyze past, present, and future time topics covered in this book, and choose what suits you best. In a rush to raise awareness, so that together we can make the society in which we live a harmonious and peaceful place, pleasing God by the work and grace of God himself"

- Oscar Pulido Fuentes

PREFACE

This book was written for those interested in humanity's well-being through POLITICS, RELIGION, and PHILOSOPHY. Philosophy is a universal science and guide to obtain wisdom. PACT provides practical, brief, and concise information to help achieve harmony between the rulers and the ruled. We will use historical antecedents from the past and present times, passages from the bible, and literature from prosperous civilizations of antiquity, such as the Jewish, the Persian, the Roman, the Egyptian, among others, to serve as references for the analysis of the current world civilization.

This read focuses on the application of POLITICS and RELIGION coexisting harmoniously in the past, the present, and the future. This harmonious application of politics and religion originated around the years 540-470 BC. And it is only possible thanks to one of the first Greek philosophers, Parmenides, and his philosophical principles, which had a tremendous impact on western and Socratic philosophy. Parmenides' principles argued that the every-day perception of reality of our physical world is mistaken. The reality in the world is, as described in Aletheia, an unchanging, everlasting, indestructible whole Being. This principle taught us that men from 20,000 years ago and today's men are essentially the same. Except for our ability to reason and develop, but the same pattern still governs our behavior. Both the social leaders of men living in caverns and the modern social leaders are the ones that guarantee economic, political, social, and cultural stability while defending their interests or that of a small group.

Suppose you accept that the goal in politics is humanity's well-being and that religions are methods created to inform humanity about God's existence to open up our hearts, have faith in God's plan, and accept that God is love. Only then will you get that if love seeks the well being of humanity, then politics and religion are similar to love. Both politics and religion are fundamental for progress, development, and faith through harmonious and peaceful transitions.

INTRODUCTION

Throughout history, our values have always been the pillar of a good society, and, to keep those same values, to protect them, to avoid devaluation, it is important to raise awareness. And for that to happen, we must have faith, hope, love, and accept that God created man in His image, male and female.

As previously mentioned, primitive men and today's men are still the same, both afraid of the unknown, adoring things or beings that we consider superior, and it has been this way since even before the Israeli became the civilization in charge of spreading the word of God by the work and grace of God himself.

Since the beginning of time, and according to his needs, men have been inventing weapons, languages, and tools. These, in general, were invented by the strong, intelligent, and wiser man, which consequently would make him the head of the hierarchy or social group. Today is no different since only the "smarter" are capable of innovation, such as creating a small camera the size of the head of a needle to watch the inside of our stomachs so we can treat an ulcer on a patient. Men have always needed other men. For that reason, we are considered social and religious beings, beings who need to be in a group to protect each other.

Fascinatingly, even primitive beings would prepare simple or complex rituals for the dead to ensure them a happy afterlife. Perhaps, instinctively, we already knew we would continue living even after death. That can only mean that primitive men also had a conscience, were capable of loving, and even in ignorance, discovered God.

Nowadays, there are millions of churches around the world practicing different religions derived from the BIBLE.

Others derived from Siddharta Gautama, also known as BUD-DHA, "The Wise," and founder of Buddhism. He ultimately died without daring to define divinity, arguing that it will only cause disunity among those who believed each man is unique and universal to decide on his existence and faith. Other religions are derived from MAHOMA, an Arab prophet founder of Islam and reformer of the polytheism of the citizens of Meca, who established the Muslim religion, giving rise to one of the most powerful religious confessions in history. Mahoma's preaching and his laws are now known as the sacred book of the Koran. But, even if we try to explain each and every religion, we would not achieve anything if you are not willing to raise awareness in the principle of tolerance and mutual respect, regardless of the cult's performance.

This book's content is intended to reach men and women, civil and religious, who want to use the power of politics and religion as practice for the common well-being of society. This book will carry the spread of emotional stability through the word of God in a written or verbal alliance between political parties, civil society, and religions regardless of the cult preference. All this for us to analyze and choose what suits the majority best and give them preference.

To achieve that, we also need to comprehend how the world is governed nowadays, or at least try, and how it deteriorates its interior government as time passes. Anarchy is only avoidable by governing Men through democracy, kings, emperors, chieftains, pharaohs, dictators, etc.; all these seek control over men for a lapse of time or even from birth until the death of the ruler in turn. A great example will be the Queen of England, Elizabeth II, who was born, and will die, in a monarchy, since a consanguineous replacement among royalty itself has already been chosen to take the throne in the event of her death. But, what price should English people and the rest of the world pay for this monarchy? We will discuss monarchies later.

First and foremost, I am Mexican; thus, our interest shifts toward another form of government, a DEMOCRACY, although, at times, one may struggle to see it as such if we take into consideration Isaiah's words:

For the leaders of the people have misled them. They have led them down the path of destruction. Therefore the lord takes no pleasure in the young men, nor will he pity the widows and fatherless, for everyone is ungodly and wicked, and they all speak foolishness. Yet for all this, his anger is not turned away, his fist is still poised to strike. This wickedness is like a brushfire; it burns not only briers and thorns but also sets the forest ablaze. Its burning sends up clouds of smoke. The land will be blackened by the fury of God and his heaven armies. The people will be fuel for the fire, and no one will spare even his own brother. They will attack their neighbor on the right but still be hungry, they will devour their neighbor on the left but still not be satisfied. In the end they will even eat their own children. Manasseh devours Ephraim and Ephraim devours Manasseh, and both will devour Judah. But God's anger will not be satisfied. His fist is still poised to strike.

(Isaiah 9:16-21)

Now, if we focus all this on Mexico's government, at a federal, state, and city-level, then:

You better believe that the in-term President, governors, local deputies, mayors, trustees, alderman, and public officials, will look huge in the next election. Mexico's political system has dominated the attention of the national life in this country for decades. Elections are held every three and six years depending on the position, and the contestants are elected through direct citizen voting and in a plurinominal way.

If we analyze the behavior and surroundings of several of the past presidents of the United States of Mexico, we will realize he suffers from vices, as do the governors and mayors, only on a smaller scale.

In Mexico, the presidents are considered deities, close to being a living God. They are granted such immense power that it is hard for a simple mortal not to get involved in flattery and worship. To get a better idea of how this government works, the elected President becomes the boss of all armed institutions in charge of keeping order in the country. The President is also the leader of the winning party that led him to power, and he dictates members' salaries, which come from the nation's federal, state, and city budgets. He decides how the national budget will be spent and how much goes to each state, making him the boss of all governors. In the congress and the senate, all bills proposed by his party will pass, even if it is something as ridiculous as growing tomatoes on the moon, because they will argue moon tomato juice is better, and they know best. The rich will send incredulous amounts of flattery and gifts to remind him they are anxiously waiting to collect what they invested in the newly-elected President's campaign. The President has a cabinet in charge of helping him maintain a presidential look, praising his intelligence, portraying him as the most patriotic, most educated person in charge of South America before the world's eyes. In conclusion, this cabinet creates the illusion of a perfect democracy in the nation. Mass media, such as TV, radio, and newspapers, are manipulated at will because of large sums of multi-million pesos paid to praise the President's vocation of service and dedication to the people. His family and friends are capable of donating a kidney in an altruistic act to the daughter of a clandestine criminal, as long as the altruistic act is recognized and praised at a national level. They want to demonstrate they are the kindest, best-intentioned, best spoken, overdressed, good looking, and that they also possess a sixth sense that will help create bills to make his term an ultimate one-of-kind form of government.

At the same time, the President gives hope to more than 4 of the strongest political groups by telling them he needs to start preparing his successor right away. All this keeps them from giving him problems after his term expires, and this kind of friendly fire happens even in the simplest work areas to keep them as alliances and maintain a balance. This game causes society to get ignorant and discouraged so that they start electing solely because the candidate is the President's best friend. After all, they are friends with a world power leader, or simply even because of pure good looks. In reality, the next leader will be the one with the broadest social network in the game, the one who can guarantee checks and balances, an equilibrium between power and money in the leading political parties.

As for the cabinet in charge of making the president look the most presidential, the one previously mentioned. Their other task is to praise those seeking to become the "successor," and it is almost unbelievable they accomplish this with a simple "the president loved your proposed bill" accompanied by a smirk and a happy look. By doing this, they create an atmosphere of deception and start a simulation to distract these men and women from their real task, reforming, developing, and making plans to create a better government.

"Their lives became full of every kind of wickedness, sin, greed, hate, envy, murder, quarreling, deception, malicious behavior and gossip. They are backstabbers, haters of God, insolent, proud, and boastful. They invent new ways of sinning, and they disobey their parents."
(Romans 1:29-30)

Every time the presidential term begins approaching its end, the presidential power starts fading as well. It is a light that lasts six years or depending on the country. Once a new successor candidate comes, the president in term stops feeling like a living god. He only then starts to feel guilt and remorse; he has failed his country, all his defects and vices are now noticeable, he was a sicko, a thief, shameless, the ones that praised him before disowned him. However, ironically, he is still untouchable. The laws and agreed values established during his term make it this way, knowing he achieved indiscriminate wealth.

And if, for a second, we think all this happens only in Mexico, we are utterly wrong. It happens in The United States of America, Brazil, Chile, Uganda, Egypt, Tunisia, Bulgaria, Spain, Portugal, Corea, Taiwan, etc. Whether we call it a Democracy, "the system," or "the game," it is only one of many systems designed to keep social stability, designed to create conditions for harmonious and peaceful transitions, so the governed yield to the rulers, and vice versa. Therefore, when such a system is interrupted or broken, violence erupts, social stability is lost, and consequently, our country and faith's development comes to a halt.

AUTHOR'S WORDS

"READER, the world we now live in developed in such a way that we are allowed to read this type of book, had it gone in any other way, everything might be different. For instance, consider that Cleopatra had no electricity, even with all her might and influence, and you do, Christopher Colombus, despite all his fame and glory, did not have a smartphone, and you do. READER, please give thanks to God for everything you have. You have no idea how blessed you are. Let us honor Mohandas Karamchand Gandhi or "Mahatma" (1869-1948), who achieved India's independence from English tyranny through peaceful resistance. Gandhi was smart enough to understand that, by force or violence, England would not hesitate to obliterate them from the face of the earth. Learn from this and make the political, social, economic, and cultural work a practice of peace and harmony, respecting and tolerating our neighbors. By doing all this, and with faith, men will achieve their purpose, be an unchanging, everlasting, indestructible Being, in simpler words, to be a unique, eternal, and continuous Being.

Distinguished Italian political writer, Niccolo Machiavelli (1467-1527), best known for his literary work "THE PRINCE" and "THE ART OF WAR," once said, "No wise man ever censured the use of an extraordinary procedure to found a kingdom or organize a republic, when the deed accuses the founder, the results it yields will excuse him." Meaning that it is okay to censor violence that destroys, but not violence that builds, or as we say nowadays, "The end justifies the means." Niccolo's way of thinking led his enemies to believe he was an evil man, just because his intelligence was far superior to those in his surroundings.

Such intelligence was believed to be a gift to subdue men in a fine and elegant way.

Before we conclude with this introduction, I would like to invite you, if so should you decide, to raise your awareness in order to grow personally and spiritually by reaching out to Political, Religious, and Philosophical protagonists in this book and your communities, they will listen to you and, more importantly, understand you".

-The Author

CHAPTER 1
THE ORIGIN OF MAN, BIBLICAL AND SCIENTIFIC

THE CREATION OF PLANET EARTH

In the beginning, God created the heavens and the earth. The earth was without form and empty, and darkness was over the surface of the deep waters. And the spirit of God was hovering over the face of the waters.

Then God said, "Let there be light", and there was light. And God saw that the light was good. Then God separated the light from the darkness. God called the light Day, and the darkness Night. And evening passed and morning came, marking the first day.

Then God said,"Let there be a space between waters, to separate the waters of the heavens from the waters of the earth". And God made the expanse and separated the waters that were under the expanse from the waters that were above the expanse. And it was so. And God called the expanse heaven. And evening passed and morning came, marking the second day.
(Genesis 1: 1-8)

The authors that wrote about the universe being created in seven days wrote it centuries before the time of Christ. In those times, they did not have telescopes to observe our stars and galaxies. They could not explain the existence of viruses and bacteria because microscopes were invented centuries after. So, the composition of everything starts with FAITH in something that has not been created yet. Therefore science itself needs to be observed in many cases with FAITH. We will explain the interrelation of these two throughout the course of this book, starting with the creation of the earth in seven days according to science.

The Bible does not specify how much time passes between each day. For all we know, it could have been billions of years. It is not about negating the Bible, but about having FAITH, and at the same time to not ignore facts nor diminish science, which naturally seeks to expose the Bible. It is about the interrelation between both, knowing that the truth is found within us and we can perceive it however we want to.

The interrelation between the BIBLICAL first two days and the Big Bang Theory is FAITH because neither has been proven. Is the beginning of time a part of the time within eternity itself? Suddenly, a big bang approximately 14 billion years ago emitted a massive energy blast capable of creating a universe, with an infinite number of galaxies within, each with their respective solar systems and an endless number of planets. How many planets? It's a mystery. How many of those planets are inhabited? Also, a mystery.

Let us concentrate on Earth. Science tells us Earth came to be approximately 4.5 billion years ago, and from its formation until today, the Earth has undergone many changes. The first stages, from when solidification of the incandescent mass began until the appearance of the Earth's crust, left no evidence of ever happening because the rocks that generated the crust remelted or were simply swallowed by a new eruption, science says, with a lot of FAITH.

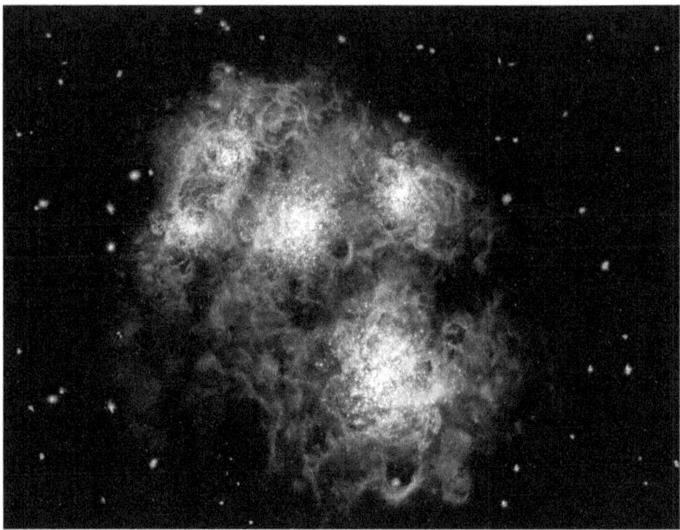

Astronomers Find One of the Youngest and Brightest Galaxies in the Early Universe by *Credit:* NASA [http://www.nasa.gov/]

Description: This is an artist's impression of an embryonic galaxy brimming with star birth in the early universe, less than a billion years after the Big Bang. The galaxy is still forming and looks nothing like the majestic spiral and elliptical galaxies that are neighbors of our Milky Way Galaxy. The illustration shows several tight clusters of stars bursting to life. They are surrounded by glowing bubbles of hydrogen gas produced by massive stars erupting as supernovae. A tapestry of young, developing galaxies is in the background. The Hubble and Spitzer space telescopes discovered a young star-forming galaxy like the one in this illustration.

THE MAN APPEARS

The following chart is shown to locate ourselves in the Geological History of the Earth and understand the condition in which we currently live in the Phanerozoic Eon, the Cenozoic Era, the Quaternary Period, and the Holocene Epoch.

Years	Eón	Era	Period	Epoch
4,500,000,000	Precambrian	Azoic		
3,800,000,000		Archaic		
2,500,000,000		Proterozoic		
560,000,000	Phanerozoic	Paleozoic	Cambric	
510,000,000			Ordovic	
438,000,000			Silurian	
408,000,000			Devonian	
360,000,000			Carboniferous	
286,000,000			Permian	
248,000,000		Mesozoic	Triassic	
213,000,000			Jurassic	
144,000,000			Cretaceous	
65,000,000		Cenozoic	Tertiary	Paleocene
56,500,000				Eocene
35,400,000				Oligocene
24,000,000				Miocene
5,200,000				Pliocene
1,600,000			Quaternary	Pleistocene
10,000				Holocene

And God said, "Let the waters under the heavens be gathered together into one place, and let the dry land appear." And it was so. God called the dry land Earth, and the waters that were gathered together he called Seas. And God saw that it was good.

And God said, "Let the earth sprout vegetation, plants yielding seed, and fruit trees bearing fruit in which is their seed, each according to its kind, on the earth." And it was so.

The earth brought forth vegetation, plants yielding seed according to their own kinds, and trees bearing fruit in which is their seed, each according to its kind. And God saw that it was good. And there was evening and there was morning, marking the third day.

And God said, "Let there be lights in the expanse of the heavens to separate the day from the night. And let them be signs to mark the seasons, and for days and years. And there was evening and there was morning, marking the fourth day.
(Genesis 1:9-14)

And God said, "Let the waters swarm with swarms of living creatures, and let birds fly above the earth across the expanse of the heavens."

And God blessed them, saying, "Be fruitful and multiply and fill the waters in the seas, and let birds multiply on the earth."And there was evening and there was morning, marking the fifth day.
(Genesis 1: 20, 22-23)

And God said, "Let the earth bring forth living creatures according to their kinds—livestock and creeping things and beasts of the earth according to their kinds." And it was so.
(Genesis 1:24)

Then God said, "Let us make man in our image, after our likeness. And let them have dominion over the fish of the sea and over the birds of the heavens and over the livestock and over all the earth and over every creeping thing that creeps on the earth."

So God created man in his own image, in the image of God he created him; male and female he created them.

And God blessed them. And God said to them, "Be fruitful and multiply and fill the earth and subdue it, and have dominion over the fish of the sea and over the birds of the heavens and over every living thing that moves on the earth." And God saw everything that he had made, and behold, it was very good.

And there was evening and there was morning, the sixth day.
(Genesis 1:26-28,31)

Thus the heavens and the earth were finished, and all the host of them. On the seventh day God had finished his work of creation, so he rested from all his work.

This is the account of the creation of the heavens and the earth. When the LORD God made the earth and the heavens.
(Genesis 2:1-2,4)

In the days following the second, according to the bible, from the third to the sixth day, millions of years also passed. Science says that the first Skillful Man, the Homo Habilis, appeared 2.4 million years ago. They were the first to make stone tools.

1.6 million years ago, in the Pleistocene Epoch, there lived the Homo Erectus, or Erect Man, who was the first to extend beyond Africa. It is said that the desire to populate the earth and the wandering characteristics of Homo Erectus are still characteristics of the current world man. During this Epoch, the ice age occurred, and during this time, numerous species, such as the saber-tooth tiger, the mammoth, among others, became extinct, making it the last event of this Epoch.

There appeared Plants and animals you currently know, such as wheat, rice, tomato, goats, cows, horses, etc., and at last the man, in the image and likeness of God, whom God knows and who knows about God. All this happens at the beginning of The Holocene Epoch, which is the most current.

The Holocene Epoch began about 10,000 years ago. The thawing of snow and ice caused the sea level to rise, invading large areas of the earth and widening Europe and the Americas' continental shelf. In general, it is a period of warm climate in which the current geographical distributions of flora and fauna are established. Human beings began to organize themselves into social groups and interrelate hunting and fishing with agriculture and livestock. This led to the stagnation and abandonment of nomadic life and the creation of the first civilizations.

The man begins to have DOMAIN over plants and animals, DOMESTICATE THEM, and mark SEASONS, days, and years. It is the present time according to Genesis in the bible. The Man made all this possible by having FAITH.

READER, you will have to discern between what the bible says and what the science says. If you choose SCIENCE, you will become dust when you die, and nothing will remain, but your FAITH in God will make you ETERNAL in SPIRIT. The wisest thing you can do is learn to live with both ideas, generating a respectable framework so that your convictions are respected.

Gothic Bible (Vulgate). Publication date c. 1275-1300
Usage CCO 1.0 Universal. Topics Medieval Art

Biblical manuscripts were highly prized and important possessions of churches, monasteries, cathedral schools, and universities throughout medieval Europe. The biblical texts were known as the vulgate, the translations made by Saint Jerome in the fourth century from Hebrew and Greek into Latin, which became the definitive and official Latin version of the Roman Church. In the 13th century, the bible was, for the first time, produced as a single volume with an officially sanctioned sequence to its books and chapters as illustrated by this example. The very extensive decoration of this bible is arranged hierarchically to indicate the relative importance of the various texts so that full or almost full-page initials mark the openings of the first prologue, Genesis, and the first Gospel; historiated initials mark the beginning of each book and illuminated initials mark the Prologues.

CHAPTER 2
ABRAHAM

A BIBLICAL PATRIARCH

To relate to the Biblical Patriarch, also known as The Father of FAITH and by the name of Abraham, we need to go back in time to the years 6000 B.C. to a region between the Euphrates River and the Tigris River called Mesopotamia, one of the six oldest civilizations in the world. The others are Egypt, China, India, Anahuac, and the Andean zone. However, we will only consider Mesopotamia solely because Abraham's ancestors come from this civilization.

Due to its geographical location between the two rivers mentioned above, Mesopotamia was all very fertile land, so the man began to dedicate himself to agriculture and livestock, leaving nomadic life behind and establishing Abraham's civilization.

When the man started living in more confined spaces, they needed to design the first urbanity rules. The Sumerians being the "most intelligent" at the time, were the first ones to create an administrative system giving rise to what we now call POLITICS. However, political systems first appeared tentatively and through FAITH around 3500 B.C

Later, around 3300 B.C., essential discoveries such as the wheel and writing were unveiled; writing on clay tablets brought the copper age, giving rise to the URUK period. But, let's skip ahead to 2350 B.C. to the times of Sargon, an Akkadian who conquered all Sumerian cities and gave rise to the first ancient empire. This marked the decaying of Sumerian language and culture, and the beginning of the Akkadian empire. This epoch was called the Akkadian Period.

In 2220 B.C., the Akkadian empire was invaded and defeated by Amorites and Guties, nomadic barbarian tribes, who imposed authority on existing city-states and created a constant state of disorder and abuse. This epoch became to be known as the Barbarian Period.

Years later, in 2100 B.C., the king of Uruk, Utu-hengal, defeated and expelled the Gutis rulers from Sumerian lands. Uruk's success would not last long, since the king of UR, Ur-Nammu would finally achieve unification of the entire region soon after. Thus the so-called III UR Dynasty came into existence, giving rise to the Summer Renaissance. In this epoch, city-states reemerged, but this time better structured with numerous written codes.

The son and heir of Ur-Nammu, Shulgi, was noted for promoting an evolution regarding weights and measures. Shulgi passed down his power to his children. Eventually, the last of his heirs, Ibbi-Sin, would be defeated by the Amorites from Arabia in 2003 B.C., marking the fall of the last Sumerian empire.

Henceforth, it would be the previously defeated Akkadian culture that would predominate, so that later, Babylon would inherit the role of such a great Summerian Empire.

In 2000 B.C., and through "FAITH," since we can't prove it, Abraham was born in a Babylonian culture in the city of U.R., located south of what is now known today as Iraq. But, what is the Biblical lineage of Abraham? The Bible says:

"The LORD God took the man and put him in the garden of Eden to work it and keep it. But the LORD God warned him, "You may freely eat the fruit of every tree in the garden—except the tree of the knowledge of good and evil. If you eat its fruit, you are sure to die." (Genesis 2:15-17)

"You won't die!" the serpent replied to the woman. "For God knows that when you eat of it your eyes will be opened, and you will be like God, knowing good and evil." The woman was convinced. She saw that the tree was beautiful and its fruit looked delicious, and she wanted the wisdom it would give her. So she took some of the fruit and ate it. Then she gave some to her husband, who was with her, and he ate it, too. (Genesis 3:4-6)

Right after eating the fruit of the forbidden tree, good and evil emerged. Then Adam and Eve gave birth to Cain, Abel, and Seth, spreading good and evil. Evil emerged when Cain killed Abel, and from Seth emerged good. From Seth comes Noah, who was born in the year 2,970 B.C., and when Noah was 600 years old, God started a universal flood to punish humanity for becoming completely corrupted; they had to be eliminated.

For those who don't believe in the UNIVERSAL FLOOD, let's analyze the following data:

The HINDU FLOOD: In India's Vedic scriptures, a king named Manu was warned by a gigantic fish of a deluge caused by the ocean waters at the bottom of the universe.

The GREEK FLOOD: This flood was produced by Poseidon, the god of the sea in Greek mythology, following Zeus' orders. Ruler of all gods, Zeus, had decided to end human existence after humanity accepted the fire Prometheus had stolen from Mount Olympus. Prometheus told his son, Deucalion, and his daughter-in-law, Pyrrha, to build an ark to bring a pair of each animal, similar to the Bible's story. And, thus, they survived and once again repopulated the earth.

The AZTEC FLOOD: The Aztec manuscript, called Borgia Code, contains the history of the world divided into ages, of which the last ended with a great deluge at the hands of the Goddess Chalchitlicue.

The INCA FLOOD: In Inca mythology, today known as Peru, the Goddess Viracocha destroyed the giants with a great flood. The two survivors, Manco Capac and Mama Ocllo repopulated the earth. They survived in sealed caves.

The MOUSSAYE FLOOD: In the African region of Chad, the Moussaye tribe in its mythology wrote that a woman, while grinding grains, raised her hand and made a hole in the sky, which was very low at the time, making it rain for 7 (seven) days and nights until the earth was flooded. As the rain fell, the sky rose until it reached the unattainable height it now has.

The TAINO FLOOD: Hieroglyphics found in San Juan, Puerto Rico, indicate that a Taino God created a great flood. And it is said that they were saved because they stayed in the river forest of Yunque.

The GUARANI FLOOD: In South America's mythology, it is said that men and gods coexisted freely in what they called the First Earth. There were no diseases nor hardships, but it all ended when incest was committed amongst them, so they were destroyed by a great flood, and the Gods set out for their heavenly home. Ñamandu, the main God of the Guarani, decided to create the Second Earth, where disease, suffering, and death now exist, for the survivors to inhabit.

By analyzing all of this, we realize that civilizations across all the continents of Earth talk about floods. All in their distinct theological way.

By tracing the ancestor lineage to Abraham, we have that he comes from Shem, son of Noah, the good one that knows and obeys the law of God. Cam, another of Noah's sons, is the one that does not obey God. This side populated Sodom and Gomorrah, cities destroyed by God due to their inhabitants' degree of decomposition.

Graphic illustration depicting The Universal Flood

PUBLIC ADMINISTRATION IN THE TIMES OF ABRAHAM

Terah took Abraham , his son, and Lot, the son of Haran, and his daughter-in-law, his son Abraham 's wife, and they left together from the Ur of the Chaldeans to go into the land of Canaan, but when they came to Haran, they settled there. Terah lived 205 years and died while still in Haran.
(Genesis 11: 31-32)

During that time and before leaving for Canaan, the Ur was ruled by king Nimrod, a worshiper of idolatry, and Abraham's father, Terah, commercialized idols, something that displeased Abraham.

Terah would socialize at King Nimrod's court and soon realized that the King wanted to kill Abraham just for having notorious leadership skills. However, Terah's heart was closer to his son than to the King; his "FAITH" in idols was undermined and collapsed within him. Moreover, because of Abraham, every day he saw suspicious looks in the other ministers' eyes, and he constantly feared for his life and that of his family.

Note that Abraham's father had one of the highest social positions of his time, combined with Abraham's notorious leadership skills, represented a POLITICAL competition for king Nimrod and his descendants.

One day, incognito, Terah went to visit Abraham, and together they decided to leave in search of a calmer country, life, and FAITH.

Terah's words for his son Abraham were: "Today I know, dear son, that you are not acting on your own, but instead out of inspiration from the Lord of heaven and earth, in whom I also believe." Abraham prayed to God, "You are my only God, in your hands I put my life and projects, guard my ways and guide my steps."

The LORD had said to Abraham, "Go from your country and your kindred and your father's house to the land that I will show you. And I will make you into a great nation, and I will bless you and make your name great, so that you will be a blessing to others. I will bless those who bless you and curse those who treat you with contempt. All the families on earth will be blessed through you. So Abraham departed as the LORD had instructed, and Lot went with him. Abraham was seventy-five years old when he left Haran. He took his wife, Sarah, his nephew Lot, and all his wealth, his livestock and all the people he had taken into his household at Haran, and headed for the land of Canaan.
(Genesis 12:1-5)

Abraham was a rich man, which caused others to follow him, not only because of his spiritual connection with God but also because he guaranteed economic, political, and social stability.

When Abraham and those who accompanied him arrived in Canaan, they noticed the inhabitants of these lands worshiped idols like Baal and Asherah. Abraham and his people repudiated such a lifestyle; thus, they aimlessly wandered through Canaanite places like Siquen, More, Bethel, Hai, Negev, among others. At that time, a harsh famine, caused by the lack of food for Abraham and Lot's herd animals, along with the war conflicts of Canaan's people, struck the land of Canaan, forcing Abraham and his people to live under horrible conditions. This situation forced them to go to Egypt.

Abraham and Sarah's Journey through Canaan to Egypt.
Publication date 1567. Topics Europe, Silver, parcel gilt,
Dishes, Metropolitan Museum of Art, Metal, United Kingdom,
Gilt, Plates, Metalwork, probably British, Silver, 1567

ABRAHAM IN EGYPT

At that time a severe famine struck the land of Canaan, forcing Abraham to go down to Egypt, where he lived as a foreigner. As he was approaching the border of Egypt, Abraham said to his wife, Sarah, "Look, you are a very beautiful woman. When the Egyptians see you, they will say, 'This is his wife. Let's kill him; then we can have her!' So please tell them you are my sister. Then they will spare my life and treat me well because of their interest in you."
(Genesis 12:10-13)

Pharaoh gave Abraham many gifts because of her—sheep, goats, cattle, male and female donkeys, male and female servants, and camels. But the LORD sent terrible plagues upon Pharaoh and his household because of Sarah, Abraham's wife. So Pharaoh summoned Abraham and accused him sharply. "What have you done to me?" he demanded. "Why didn't you tell me she was your wife? Why did you say, 'She is my sister,' and allow me to take her as my wife? Now then, here is your wife. Take her and get out of here!"
(Genesis 12:16-19)

After learning that Abraham offered Sarah to Pharaoh, we could consider him as someone with questionable morals. However, it also shows the trust and confidence he had in his wife.

First of all, Sarah and Abraham were siblings of Terah, still, different mothers. Remember that marriage between blood relatives was allowed, so they did not lie to Pharaoh; they just omitted that they were married.

It's worth mentioning Abraham possessed quite a good upbringing and education, given he came from the royalty of Ur culture. His knowledge excelled in astrology, mathematics, public relations, and most importantly, he made sure to portray himself as a wealthy character everywhere he went. With this, it is easy to imagine the type of public relations discussed with the Pharaoh when they arrived in Egypt. Pharaoh had an expansionist policy in effect, a situation that favored Abraham due to the extent of the cultural exchange that the Pharaoh demanded, since Abraham knew the Merchant Routes from Mesopotamia to Cannan and from the Caspian sea to the Mediterranean Sea.

The ego of Pharaohs in Egypt was directed to leaving an architectural legacy during their reigns, whether it be pyramids, monuments, statues, or anything that distinguished him. Abraham knew mathematics and astrology, fundamental sciences in the practice of architecture. It is believed that this is why Abraham did so well in Egypt, rather than because of the beauty of Sarah, remember she was ten years younger than Abraham, and when they left Haran, Abraham was 75 years old. Therefore, Sarah would be in her late sixties around this time. Although she had not been a mother and had remained conserved, she resembled an older woman, who, as a concubine of Pharaoh, did not awaken a great carnal desire. For that, he had more beautiful and younger women than Sarah. However, it is believed Sarah married the Pharaoh for only one reason, that is to establish an alliance between Egypt and the Chaldeans in Ur since Sarah had royal lineage from her father, Terah, also the father of Abraham.

Pharaoh was interested in Egypt's trade with Mesopotamia, passing through Canaan. But when he realized Sarah was married and the suffering caused by the plagues in Egypt, he lost interest. He told Abraham to take his wife, their possessions and leave. It's worth mentioning that the Pharaoh had built a great friendship with Abraham, who would tell him about God, a God very different from the Pharaoh's Gods. The misfortunes brought by the plagues to Egypt are a product of Abraham 's God's punishment, Pharaoh believed, so he said, "go and take yours," being a politician. He wanted to remain on good terms with Canaan and Mesopotamia, two cultures heavily influenced by Abraham.

God planned all this with one purpose in mind, the formation of Abraham, teaching him the constitution of people as a society so that he could educate them to spread his word and his FAITH as the nation of Abraham.

ABRAHAM IN CANAAN

So Abraham left Egypt and traveled north into the Negev, along with his wife and Lot and all that they owned. Abraham had become very wealthy in livestock and in silver and gold. From the Negev, they continued traveling by stages toward Bethel, and they pitched their tents between Bethel and Ai, where they had camped before. to the place where he had made an altar at the first. And there Abraham called upon the name of the LORD.

(Genesis 13:1-4)

It is easy to understand that Abraham had only become wealthy in silver and gold because, unlike livestock, only people with royal lineage could own precious metals. Such metals guaranteed social distinction among the inhabitants of Canaan. Most ordinary people had cattle, but only kings and members of their courts could wear jewelry on their bodies. Abraham knew perfectly well all of this, he had a formative profile as a politician, and as a politician, he had to conquer Canaan in communion with God.

Then the king of Sodom, the king of Gomorrah, the king of Admah, the king of Zeboiim and the king of Bela (that is, Zoar) marched out and drew up their battle lines in the Valley of Siddim against Kedorlaomer king of Elam, Tidal king of Goyim, Amraphel king of Shinar and Arioch king of Ellasar--four kings against five.

(Genesis 14:8-9)

The victorious invaders then plundered Sodom and Gomorrah and headed for home, taking with them all the spoils of war and the food supplies. They also took Abraham's nephew

Lot and his possessions, since he was living in Sodom. But one of Lot's men escaped and reported everything to Abraham the Hebrew, who was living near the oak grove belonging to Mamre the Amorite. Mamre and his relatives, Eshcol and Aner, were Abraham's allies   (Genesis 14:11-13)

Abraham knew that there had always been alliances with the natives of the conquered land in every conquest. He followed a basic manual on expansionism, one used in Egypt by Pharaoh, who befriended Abraham and possibly instructed him on the art of conquest.

When Abraham heard that his nephew Lot had been captured, he mobilized the 318 trained men who had been born into his household. Then he pursued Kedorlaomer's army until he caught up with them at Dan.
(Genesis 14:14)

Abraham was a wealthy man, one who could easily afford to pay for someone to discipline his men in the art of conquest. Men disciplined to follow his plans and act on behalf of his "FAITH."

The one most interested in Abraham's success in Canaan was Egypt since Canaan had experts in trade with the middle east, the great Mesopotamia, a region of many riches, mostly food, highly coveted by the merchants.

And there Abraham said of his wife Sarah, "She is my sister." Then Abimelech king of Gerar sent for Sarah and took her.
(Genesis 20:2)

Sarah was now over 85 years old. It is believed that the only reason Abimelech, the Philistine king, took her as his wife was to create a political alliance with the Hebrews. But after realizing that she was already married, in a revelation of God through a dream, he understood that this would not be possible.

Abraham said, "I did it because I thought, 'There is no fear of God at all in this place', and they will kill me because of my wife."
(Genesis 20:11)

Abimelech feared the GOD of Abraham, for he saw how he

rescued Lot and killed his captors; Abraham was accompanied by God himself.

Then Abimelech took some of his sheep and goats, cattle, and male and female servants, and he presented them to Abraham. He also returned his wife, Sarah, to him. Then Abimelech said, "Look over my land and choose any place where you would like to live."

And he said to Sarah, "Look, I am giving your 'brother' 1,000 pieces of silver in the presence of all these witnesses. This is to compensate you for any wrong I may have done to you. This will settle any claim against me, and your reputation is cleared." (Genesis 20:14-16)

God's plan, "the conquest of the lands of Canaan," began to be fulfilled through Abraham.

An alliance was formed between Abimelech and Abraham, not under Abimelech's terms, but how God and Abraham intended.

Now, it was time for God to fulfill the PACT he had with Abraham. His descendants would be born, starting with Isaac, then with Jacob, who eventually fathered Joseph, who became vizier, the second most powerful man in Egypt next to Pharaoh.

Time would continue to pass in the evolution of administrative disciplines of the people of Israel. Throughout the Exodus, Leviticus, Numbers, and Deuteronomy with Moises. Until Judges, when they constituted themselves as a society with a discipleship profile. That was God's plan to build the nation he wanted.

Thus, marking the era of the Kings of Israel, 1000 years after Abraham. Kings who knew of God and God knew of them.

REFLECTION 1

Instruct the wise, and they will be even wiser. Teach the righteous, and they will learn even more. The fear of the LORD is the beginning of wisdom, and the knowledge of the Holy One is insight. (Proverbs 9-10)

It is in our thinking where we can generate changes to become successful thinkers. All the successful men and women you know are distinguished by one thing: "Positive thinking. "

Ask yourself this question, Do you want personal success? If so, start by convincing yourself that it will cost you time, concentration, and effort, all in necessary doses to achieve the goals you set for yourself. How you prepare your mind and how you act will amount to the size of your reward.

Prepare to understand that your brain does not accept the word 'NO.' For instance, if you tell a child, "Don't run across the street," the child will run across. However, if you say to a child, "Cross the street slowly and carefully," the message changes, and the child begins to visualize it better.

Success is never given; you have to earn it. You must have a positive attitude, which is the most important thing to carry out any project we may have.

Fear of failure will always be the biggest obstacle when trying to accomplish something. Poverty in mind and soul is worse than lack of money. You can be rich or poor, healthy or sick, happy or miserable. It all depends on your attitude.

All of us can give a better meaning to our life, it all depends on our attitude. It is imperative to visualize what we want and apply ourselves to it. WE want the best use of our CHRISTIAN heritage in governments. That is what this book is for, to discipline ourselves in **FAITH** and **Public Administration.**

CHAPTER 3
DAVID

A BIBLICAL KING

When Samuel became old, he made his sons judges over Israel. The name of his firstborn son was Joel, and the name of his second, Abijah; they were judges in Beersheba. Yet his sons did not walk in his ways but turned aside after gain. They took bribes and perverted justice.

(1 Samuel 8:1-3)

Samuel is the last Biblical Judge, also considered a Prophet. At that time, the type of government was THEOCRATIC, in other words, "the Power of God. " Samuel himself wanted to continue the tradition of these governments, inheriting power to his children, but that was not the plan of God. The Almighty God knew that the people of Israel, in their social spheres, were degraded entirely, that the children of Samuel were wicked and corrupt. However, they were precisely the rulers the people deserved. It was time to enter the MONARCHIES, civilizations ruled by KINGS and their descendants. Israel had to evolve to catch up to the ECONOMIC, POLITICAL, and SOCIAL status of other nations.

As the sons of Samuel ruled Israel, a great event occurred. DAVID was born. In the year 1040 B.C. approximately.

FIRST KING OF ISRAEL

Finally, all the elders of Israel met at Ramah to discuss the matter with Samuel. "Look," they told him, "you are now old, and your sons are not like you. Give us a king to judge us like all the other nations have."
(1 Samuel 8:4-5)

That must have been very hard for Samuel as a father, a Judge, and a Prophet since the people he had served his entire life were now asking for his resignation as a Lifetime Judge, which included any power his children had. However, Samuel was a man that feared God, and that is where his wisdom came from. When he consulted the request of his people with God, God said, "if they want a KING, give them one."

Then Samuel took a flask of olive oil and poured it over Saul's head. He kissed Saul and said, "I am doing this because the LORD has appointed you to be the ruler over Israel, his special possession.
(1 Samuel 10:1)

These events marked the transition of powers, from Judges to Kings, but, as we know, resistance to change happens everywhere, and Israel was not going to be an exception. There were supporters of the Judges who wanted to stay in power and keep their privileges, and supporters of the KINGS because they wanted that power and those privileges for themselves.

Then the people exclaimed to Samuel, "Now where are those men who said, 'Why should Saul rule over us?' Bring them here, and we will kill them!"

But Saul replied, "No one will be executed today, for today the LORD has rescued Israel!".

Then Samuel said to the people, "Come, let us all go to Gilgal to renew the kingdom."

So they all went to Gilgal, and in a solemn ceremony before the LORD they made Saul king. Then they offered peace offerings to the LORD, and Saul and all the Israelites were filled with joy. **(1 Samuel 11: 12-15)**

This act is one of the most important POLITICAL PACTS seen in the Old testament. Samuel's sons were among those who did not love the Kings. And Saul was already a King anointed by Samuel. In those understood values in politics, Samuel, being a judge, when handing over power to Saul, asked him to spare his children's lives, and Saul granted it.

The plan God had in store for these characters began to develop. He had to educate people to go from a THEOCRATIC administration ruled by judges to MONARCHIES ruled by Kings. This transition needed to happen gradually, which is why Samuel was indispensable to Saul while ruling over Israel. Saul knew that the people of which he was King, was inhabited not only by HEBREWS but by other communities, such as the Philistines, the Amorites, etc., and the last thing they needed was division between the Israelites. They had reached the highest level of government known at the time. Finally, Israel was theirs, of the Hebrews, the people God wanted to represent him before all nations. The next step was to place a King to do what God commanded.

SAUL'S FAILURE

The Philistines mustered to fight Israel, a mighty army of 3,000 chariots, 6,000 charioteers, and as many warriors as the grains of sand on the seashore! They camped at Michmash east of Beth-aven.
(1 Samuel 13:5)

And some Hebrews crossed the fords of the Jordan to the land of Gad and Gilead. Saul was still at Gilgal, and all the people followed him trembling.

Saul waited there seven days for Samuel, as Samuel had instructed him earlier, but Samuel still didn't come. Saul realized that his troops were rapidly slipping away.

So he demanded, "Bring me the burnt offering and the peace offerings!" And Saul sacrificed the burnt offering himself.

Just as Saul was finishing with the burnt offering, Samuel arrived. Saul went out to meet and welcome him,

but Samuel said, "What is this you have done?" Saul replied, "I saw my men scattering from me, and you didn't arrive when you said you would, and the Philistines are at Michmash ready for battle.

So I said, 'The Philistines are ready to march against us at Gilgal, and I haven't even asked for the LORD's help!' So I felt compelled to offer the burnt offering myself before you came."

"How foolish!" Samuel exclaimed. "You have not kept the command the LORD your God gave you. Had you kept it, the LORD would have established your kingdom over Israel forever.

But now your kingdom must end, for the LORD has sought out a man after his own heart. The LORD has already appointed him to be the leader of his people, because you have not

kept the LORD's command."
(1 Samuel 13:7-14)

When this happened, it broke the relationship between Saul and Samuel because Saul had performed the offering, which was Samuel's task, and by doing this, he was ignoring the power Samuel still had as a living judge and as a man known by God. In the following years, Samuel would be in charge of looking for a King God himself would point out to him, a king who would learn from Saul's mistakes, and who would modify the way of governing, a King that would do things as God wanted, not as he believed them to be.

Until the day Samuel died, he did not go to see Saul again, though Samuel mourned for him. And the LORD regretted that he had made Saul king over Israel.
(1 Samuel 15:35)

Now the LORD said to Samuel, "You have mourned long enough for Saul. I have rejected him as king of Israel, so fill your flask with olive oil and go to Bethlehem. Find a man named Jesse who lives there, for I have selected one of his sons to be my king."

But Samuel asked, "How can I do that? If Saul hears about it, he will kill me." "Take a heifer with you," the LORD replied, "and say that you have come to make a sacrifice to the LORD."
(1 Samuel 16:1-2)

For comfort, Samuel was happy with the position assigned to him by Saul, but the people of Israel had lost track of God. Samuel had to choose; either he kept the comfort he had with King Saul or confronted him. Yet God trusted him, and Samuel did the right thing by doing what he commanded.

And Jesse made seven of his sons pass before Samuel. And Samuel said to Jesse, "The LORD has not chosen these."

Then Samuel asked, "Are these all the sons you have?" "There is still the youngest," Jesse replied. "But he's out in the fields watching the sheep and goats." "Send for him at once," Samuel said. "We will not sit down to eat until he arrives."

So Jesse sent for him. He was dark and handsome, with

beautiful eyes. And the LORD said, "This is the one; anoint him."

Then Samuel took the horn of oil and anointed him in the midst of his brothers. And the Spirit of the LORD rushed upon David from that day forward. And Samuel rose up and went to Ramah.
(1 Samuel 16:10-13)

The tradition back then was to assign the youngest of sons the simplest and most ordinary jobs. For that same reason, David was the shepherd in charge of Jesse's family's cattle, while his older brothers, not all, were soldiers of King Saul. The fact they were soldiers of the King can only mean that Jesse's family had a wealthy economic and social position since not anyone had the right to be a soldier of the King or belong to the royalty guard.

News about David heading to the royal palace to face Saul began to surface, but how would they accomplish such an act? David was only a 15 or 16-year-old shepherd.

Samuel had secretly anointed David, and this act would result in David suffering at Saul's hands. But God planned to have David learn to become a King, and only another King could teach him how. The learning would be harsh, but it was the only way to forge the discipline and character that were in accordance with the behavior of the society that inhabited that time.

Now the Spirit of the LORD had left Saul, and the LORD sent a tormenting spirit that filled him with depression and fear. (1 Samuel 16:14)

One of the servants said to Saul, "One of Jesse's sons from Bethlehem is a talented harp player. Not only that— he is a brave warrior, a man of war, and has good judgment. He is also a fine-looking young man, and the LORD is with him." **(1 Samuel 16:18)**

Samuel had people within Saul's reign who were very grateful to him. In these times, political groups already existed, Saul's group and Samuel's group. Thus, it is very likely that the servant under Saul who recommended David belonged to Samuel's political group. Somehow, he was aware of the plan in motion, so David's description was that of a well-educated boy in the highest social spheres. It is also known that the house of Jesse and Saul had good relations.

So David went to Saul and began serving him. Saul loved David very much, and David became his armor bearer.

Then Saul sent word to Jesse asking, "Please let David remain in my service, for I am very pleased with him.

And whenever the tormenting spirit from God troubled Saul, David would play the harp. Then Saul would feel better, and the tormenting spirit would go away.

(1 Samuel 16:23)

DAVID PREPARES TO BE KING

The Lord's plan for David had different stages. He knew that it had to be structured so that he could govern according to his will. For this reason, he could not expose David, for he was his chosen to be the King who would rule his people. David had to observe Saul and his ways of governing, learn the kingdom's administrative structure, how Saul ordered around, how he delegated responsibilities, how he distributed wealth, how Saul dominated his enemies, and how he rewarded loyalties. In short, David had to perfect all these practices to please God.

SAUL AND DAVID SPLIT UP

Then Goliath, a Philistine champion from Gath, came out of the Philistine ranks to face the forces of Israel. He was over nine feet tall!
(1 Samuel 17:4)

Goliath stood and shouted a taunt across to the Israelites. "Why are you all coming out to fight?" he called. "I am the Philistine champion, but you are only the servants of Saul. Choose one man to come down here and fight me! If he kills me, then we will be your slaves. But if I kill him, you will be our slaves!
(1 Samuel 17:8-9)

But David went back and forth so he could help his father with the sheep in Bethlehem.
(1 Samuel 17:15)

From the time Samuel anointed David, to the time he would face Goliath, about four or five years had passed. Unlike his older brothers, he was not the age to be a soldier of Saul. For that reason, he was free to go from the palace to his father's house. He was a young man that did not attract attention, unlike Goliath who would present himself as a warrior when he was nineteen or twenty years old. The shepherds at the service of Jesse's house would care for the herds of his father. David only supervised the family's assets since his father and family knew he would be Saul's successor. David's father sent him with loaves for his brothers, despite him knowing what was happening with Goliath and where the battle against the Philistines was taking place. Still, he figured it was time to start the power succession since the

conditions were being met. Meanwhile a rumor was spreading: **"Have you seen the giant?" the men asked. "He comes out each day to defy Israel. The king has offered a huge reward to anyone who kills him. He will give that man one of his daughters for a wife, and the man's entire family will be exempted from paying taxes!"**
(1 Samuel 17:25)

One of the world's rulers' oldest political practices is to have among their collaborators those who are going to commit themselves on the ruler's behalf. This way, whether they deliver or not, it does not matter. After all, the ruler himself did not say anything, giving him the option to evaluate the offer presented, and, whatever his decision is, he will be fine.

Reaching into his shepherd's bag and taking out a stone, he hurled it with his sling and hit the Philistine in the forehead. The stone sank in, and Goliath stumbled and fell face down on the ground.
(1 Samuel 17:49)

Then David ran over and pulled Goliath's sword from its sheath. David used it to kill him and cut off his head. When the Philistines saw that their champion was dead, they turned and ran.
(1 Samuel 17:51)

And as soon as David returned from the striking down of the Philistine, Abner took him, and brought him before Saul with the head of the Philistine in his hand. "Tell me about your father, young man," Saul said. And David replied, "His name is Jesse, and we live in Bethlehem."
(1 Samuel 17:57-58)

This episode in David's life had to be of significant impact because he had played the harp for Saul, had been his squire, and even received the uniform to fight Goliath from him, and yet he asked David who he was. Saul knew perfectly well that David was the successor of Abraham, Issac, and Jacob, that he had a whole dynasty behind him. Saul also knew he was a serious competitor to the throne, and he knew that David and his daughters had lived together in the royal palace and that his daughter Michal loved him intensely. He knew that by marrying David to his daughter, he would automatically be related to Israel's royalty. **He told them, "Tell David that all I want for the bride price is 100 Philistine foreskins! Vengeance on my enemies is all I really want." But what Saul had in mind was that David would be killed in the fight. David was delighted to accept the offer. Before the time limit expired, he and his men went out and killed 200 Philistines. Then David fulfilled the king's requirement by presenting all their foreskins to him. So Saul gave his daughter Michal to David to be his wife.**

(1 Samuel 18:25-27)

David's popularity had grown so much in the eyes of the observance of the people of Israel, so much in fact that if Saul killed him, he would be martyred, and digging his own grave, aside from being a tremendous political error. After all, the people already believed he was a bad ruler, one who did not follow God's instructions and imposed rigorous taxes. Moreover, the people noticed the group that formed part of Saul's government body had as many luxuries as possible. They wore the best skins, the best fabrics, ate the best delicacies, and drank the best wines. Their metals were gold and silver, had countless lovers, in some cases of the same sex, and practiced orgies. In short, the testimony of their conduct to the people of Israel left much to be desired. The Kingdom of Saul was in chaos. However, this was God's plan; the people of Israel had to live and experience this because they asked for a King of their own, just like other nations, pagan kings, idol worshipers, who lacked morals and principles. He had to teach them how the next King should govern over them, "not as the King wants, but as God wants."

Art of the battle between Goliath, the Philistine, and David

DAVID'S GROWTH

Saul now urged his servants and his son Jonathan to assassinate David. But Jonathan, because of his strong affection for David, told him what his father was planning. "Tomorrow morning," he warned him, "you must find a hiding place out in the fields.

(1 Samuel 19:1-2)

Jonathan, the son of Saul, born and raised in Israel's highest social spheres, was brilliant and highly educated. He knew that the people did not like his father's government, and that he had reached the highest magistracy possible, and that the only thing left for him was to descend. He also knew his father had to think about his safety and that of his family, so taking advantage of David's friendship was the most prudent and logical thing since he knew that his friend and brother-in-law would be the successor of his father's throne. For his part, David, as a political strategy, having Samuel's group on his side and dividing Saul's group through Jonathan, knew that it would only be a matter of time for Saul's general, Abner, to join his side. General Abner appreciated David for his bravery and his natural gift as a war strategist, also because he was liked by the people and loved by God.

So David left Gath and escaped to the cave of Adullam. Soon his brothers and all his other relatives joined him there. Then others began coming, men who were in trouble, in debt, or who were just discontented, until David was the captain of about 400 men.

(1 Samuel 22:1-2)

David's brothers, who previously belonged to Saul's army, had deserted, and with them many others, they no longer felt respect, honor, nor glory for King Saul. He had become a tyrant, accompanied only by those who did it out of fear, out of necessity, or simply because they were mercenaries at the service of gold and silver, by those ambitious in the pursuit of nobility and property, evil men and women, people who cared little or nothing for the people of Israel.

Given this, David would become a leader who had formed his army out of guerillas. He had no money to pay them; therefore, those who followed him wanted what was best for the people of Israel, they fought for a noble cause. They were joyful to see their leader David behave in solidarity with his people.

"Listen here, you men of Benjamin!" Saul shouted to his officers when he heard the news. "Has that son of Jesse promised every one of you fields and vineyards? Has he promised to make you all generals and captains in his army? Is that why you have all conspired against me? No one tells me when my son makes a covenant with the son of Jesse. None of you is concerned about me or tells me that my son has incited my servant to lie in wait for me, as he does today."

Then Doeg the Edomite, who was standing there with Saul's men, spoke up. "When I was at Nob," he said, "I saw the son of Jesse talking to the priest, Ahimelech, son of Ahitub. Ahimelech consulted the LORD for him; he also gave him provisions and the sword of Goliath the Philistine."
(1 Samuel 22:7-10)

It is necessary to understand that Saul, being the King, had enough land and vineyards and the power to distribute powerful positions amongst his social structures as he pleased. However, he did not distribute any of this to Benjamin's men, nor many others, but only to a few who, like him, were willing to plunder the goods of Israel for their own personal benefit or that of their small group.

The people of Benjamin and Jonathan's allies knew that they would do better with anyone other than with Saul.

In the case of the Edomite, it is a real example that when a mandate declines, one that is characterized by the bad deeds it has done, it will only keep the worst groups; those who have helped carry these terrible deeds. Those who abandoned the mandate the soonest are those who want a change for good.

Then David prayed, "O LORD, God of Israel, I have heard that Saul is planning to come and destroy Keilah because I am here. Will the leaders of Keilah betray me to him? And will Saul actually come as I have heard? O LORD, God of Israel, please tell me." And the LORD said, "He will come." Again David asked, "Will the leaders of Keilah betray me and my men to Saul?" And the LORD replied, "Yes, they will betray you." Then David and his men, who were about six hundred, arose and departed from Keilah, and they went wherever they could go. When Saul was told that David had escaped from Keilah, he gave up the expedition. (1 Samuel 23:10-13)

David knew that fear was the only thing Saul had left to use against the people of Israel to subdue it.

All the people cannot be included in the government's budget; thus, the people have to earn with good work and services. The budget must be used to pay our public servants.

David noticed that wherever he went, the people protected him; for this, he had to be careful not to compromise them to keep Saul from retaliating against them.

Every day more followers joined him, men from different towns, from different families, men who composed a social network of people who spread the word of what David wanted to do as a government. He tried to communicate with the people so they could tell him their needs. Besides just words, the people would notice how after every battle they fought and won, David would distribute everything they had seized among the men so they could then give it to their families. This only made David become more popular and loved by his followers, something Saul hated.

DAVID FORGIVES SAUL

At the place where the road passes some sheepfolds, Saul went into a cave to relieve himself. But as it happened, David and his men were hiding farther back in that very cave!

"Now's your opportunity!" David's men whispered to him. "Today the LORD is telling you, 'I will certainly put your enemy into your power, to do with as you wish.'" So David crept forward and cut off a piece of the hem of Saul's robe. But then David's conscience began bothering him because he had cut Saul's robe. He said to his men, "The LORD forbid that I should do this to my lord the king. I shouldn't attack the LORD's anointed one, for the LORD himself has chosen him."
(1 Samuel 24:3-6)

The fact that David did not want to kill Saul is proof of how much he respected God because, just like himself, Saul also had been anointed by Samuel. We know that David and Saul shared common enemies, the Philistines. They also had similarities; Samuel had anointed both by the same God's disposition. However, they represented different political interests, which placed them in rival groups. Still, if David wanted to earn the full respect of the Hebrews, as head of the group, he had to be different from Saul and unify Israel's people.

The duty to criticize or replace a bad ruler should not prevent you from respecting him nor the responsibilities that God had left him in charge of, and David, as future King, had to set an example so he would not be criticized.

Now the Philistines attacked Israel, and the men of Israel fled before them. Many were slaughtered on the slopes of Mount Gilboa. The Philistines closed in on Saul and his sons, and they

killed three of his sons—Jonathan, Abinadab, and Malkishua. The fighting grew very fierce around Saul, and the Philistine archers caught up with him and wounded him severely. Saul groaned to his armor bearer, "Take your sword and kill me before these pagan Philistines come to run me through and taunt and torture me." But his armor bearer was afraid and would not do it. So Saul took his own sword and fell on it.

(1 Samuel 31:1-4)

Thus, this marked the end of another part of the formation the Almighty had planned for Israel, one filled with terror, looting, abuse, and calamities. It was the price they had to pay for wanting a King like the ones other nations had.

They had to learn to have kings as God wanted, not as they arranged. David would become the next King in the region of Judah, in the city of Hebron. Like Saul did with Samuel, David would have to confront the groups that had the power when Saul was King, and that would oppose the change, and only through some negotiations would they accept him.

David knew that it was a matter of time to unify the people of Israel in Hebron. The people ruled by David enjoyed goods, harmony, and freedom. Thus, David became a King beloved by his people. Except by Abner, Saul's army general, who wanted to maintain his power and privileges, so he convinced Ish-bosheth, son of Saul, to become King of Israel, and like his father, rule through fear, looting, abuses, and calamities. Ish-bosheth would reign for two years.

David would reign for seven and a half years.

DAVID KING OF ISRAEL

David would soon realize that Ish-bosheth, Saul's son, was just a puppet in Abner's hands and the only obstacle remaining in Israel. Therefore if Ish-bosheth went to his side, under any method, he would win the battle. David understood well that Ish-bosheth and Abner had a cultural formation of bandits, rogues, and abusers; they could not last long together since neither of them was trustworthy. Any pretext would serve to break relations between the two of them.

Abner said: May God strike me and even kill me if I don't do everything I can to help David get what the LORD has promised him! I'm going to take Saul's kingdom and give it to David. I will establish the throne of David over Israel as well as Judah, all the way from Dan in the north to Beersheba in the south."

Ish-bosheth didn't dare say another word because he was afraid of what Abner might do.

Then Abner sent messengers to David, saying, "Doesn't the entire land belong to you? Make a solemn pact with me, and I will help turn over all of Israel to you."

"All right," David replied, "but I will not negotiate with you unless you bring back my wife Michal, Saul's daughter, when you come."

(2 Samuel 3:9-13)

Abner was a man of experience, and somehow he knew that the tribes of Israel were gathering to support David, so he had to do something to draw the attention of the one who would soon become King of all Israel. He knew that Michal, daughter of Saul, was David's wife. By bringing her before David and giving him back Saul's family's power, he was consolidating a political alliance between the two divisions of Israel, the north, governed by Ish-bosheth, and the south, governed by David. What David demanded Abner to do to agree to make a pact was to get Michal. She had been married to another man, not respecting David nor the foreskins of the Philistines he gave for her, but if Abner could rescue Michal from that commitment, he would be acknowledged by David. Abner achieved this quite easily since Michal's husband was a man of weak character, someone who knew what Abner was capable of, and if he disobeyed, it could cost him his life.

When Abner and twenty of his men came to Hebron, David entertained them with a great feast. Then Abner said to David, "Let me go and call an assembly of all Israel to support my lord the king. They will make a covenant with you to make you their King, and you will rule over everything your heart desires." So David sent Abner safely on his way.
(2 Samuel 3:20-21)

David was an excellent politician. Without spilling blood unnecessarily and making pacts with only those he needed to deal with, he acquired the territory that made him the only King of Israel and Judah.

In God's plan, Ish-bosheth and Abner just hindered David; that is why he created the conditions for both to be killed, and for his people to look up to David, people who did not represent interests that hinder the arrival to the throne of Israel. **Then all the tribes of Israel went to David at Hebron and told him, "We are your own flesh and blood. In the past, when Saul was our king, you were the one who really led the forces of Israel. And the LORD told you, 'You will be the shepherd of my people Israel. You will be Israel's leader.'" So there at Hebron, King David made a covenant before the LORD with all the elders of Israel. And they anointed him king of Israel.**
(2 Samuel 5:1-3)

This stage in the formation of David's reign over Israel is undoubtedly the most important. The northern tribes recognized him as King, and the southern tribes were with him. All that remained was to conquer Jerusalem, which was governed by the Canaanites, who, after being attacked from the north and south by David's armies, were easily defeated. Jerusalem then becomes the capital of this united kingdom. The northern tribes, in a pact they had made with David, asked to retain their luxuries and privileges; David granted this to be the unifying King of the tribes that made up the people of God. Over time David would begin implementing a government designed to please God, but many did not like it because they wanted to continue practices they exercised when Saul was King, and that would cause many conflicts and wars, conflicts between those of his blood and wars between enemies. Still, since David did everything according to God's will, those conflicts and wars would always have an outcome in David's favor.

God would give David rest from his enemies in Jerusalem, and they would pact that his descendants would rule the people of Israel. If he were to fail, God would punish him like a father punishes a son, but he would not abandon him like he abandoned Saul. And God told him one more thing: "**Your house and your kingdom will continue before me for all time, and your throne will be secure forever.**"
(2 Samuel 7:16)

KING DAVID
(The Red Bone King)

The red bone is known for having one of the most beautiful complex-ions among Black people. King David was also a redbone. The word red bone is a term that was given to a particular type of people in the Black community.

DAVID'S FAILURE

Late one afternoon, after his midday rest, David got out of bed and was walking on the roof of the palace. As he looked out over the city, he noticed a woman of unusual beauty taking a bath. He sent someone to find out who she was, and he was told, "She is Bathsheba, the daughter of Eliam and the wife of Uriah the Hittite."
(2 Samuel 11:2-3)

This woman undoubtedly awoke in King David a great desire, but since she was married, wanting to become intimate with her would condemn her to adultery. This act practically sentenced her to death.

It is vital that we become aware of the weakness and evil of which even God's friends can be victims. David arranged for Uriah, who was fighting against the Ammonites, to be killed by conspiring to place him in a vulnerable combat position through a letter that read: **"Station Uriah on the front lines where the battle is fiercest. Then pull back so that he will be killed."**
(2 Samuel 11:15)

David took Bathsheba as his wife, who eventually gave him a son. Nevertheless, what David had done WAS NOT TO GOD'S LIKING. And this would be his punishment: **Now, therefore, the sword shall never depart from your house, because you have despised me and have taken the wife of Uriah the Hittite to be your wife.'** (2 Samuel 12:10)

Then David confessed to Nathan, "I have sinned against the LORD." Nathan replied, "Yes, but the LORD has forgiven you, and you won't die for this sin. Nevertheless, because by this deed you have utterly scorned the LORD, the child who is born to you

shall die." (2 Samuel 12:13-14)

David is a perfect example of the repentant sinner. Every mistake has its consequence, and this one would cost David dearly because it would be Absalom, one of his sons, the blood of his blood, the one to cause him so much bitterness. Within his family, envy, betrayal, and evil passions would be unleashed. Peace in Jerusalem would end. It wasn't long before David forgot that God is not pleased with shallow ceremonies; he is pleased with the heart's purity and justice to our neighbor.

DAVID'S MILITARY STRUCTURES

In every government, there exists a branch, within its structure, in charge of protecting itself. David, due to his faults as a ruler, and for the fulfillment of God's will, had to face his enemies continually, that's why he gave this order: **"Go throughout the tribes of Israel from Dan to Beersheba and enroll the fighting men, so that I may know how many there are."** (2 Samuel 24:2)

David proved to be an actual statistician and military strategist, confident in his power as a King. He could easily afford to pay for that work, and yes, they conducted an army census, counting 1,300,000 men in the northern and southern tribes of Israel that could serve in his army. Once again, David offended and doubted God because, by wanting to form an army paid to defend him from his enemies, he'd be carrying practices done by Saul. The only difference was that David reconsidered and asked God for forgiveness, choosing the Almighty to be his punisher and not the men. The people of Israel then suffered a plague that killed thousands. David begged God to punish him since it was he who had sinned. God, who is all love, forgave him, and on the plot of Arauna, he built an altar. David would die full of glory, and his kingdom and his house would continue to be ruled by another king. Solomon, his son.

REFLECTION 2

The LORD told Elijah "Yet I will leave seven thousand in Israel, all the knees that have not bowed to Baal, and every mouth that has not kissed him."
(1 Kings 19:18)

The LORD told Gideon, "With these 300 men I will rescue you and give you victory over the Midianites. Send all the others home."
(Judges 7:7)

Jesus Christ Said: "I also tell you this: If two of you agree here on earth concerning anything you ask, my Father in heaven will do it for you. For where two or three gather together as my followers, I am there among them."
(Matthew 18:19-20)

The determination of the action is what evaluates the quality of the results. It is not about just working since many work very hard but never do well, for the simple reason they lack defined objectives and correct planning.

Success is not achieved just by working hard but also by using intelligence and common sense. You must ask yourself, why am I reading this book? What am I going to get out of it? Who is going to benefit from it?

Some of the answers that can help you are the following: This book will allow you to find out about the type of man or woman who wants to govern over you, and it will allow you to decide whether you grant him power or not. Bear in mind that with good rulers, you will achieve social, economic, and political stability.

We will all benefit when comprehensive development projects are carried out in our cities and towns. The better prepared we are, and with the ability to work in groups, the better the outcome will be.

Those who have carefully planned their work using the powers of concentration, observation, and imagination and also add a constant action that does not allow them to look back at any time. They will find it very difficult not to achieve what they have planned.

CHAPTER 4
JESUS CHRIST

KING OF KINGS

Jesus, son of Mary and Joseph, was a direct descendant of Abraham, Isaac, Jacob, David, etc., a complete tradition in the people of Israeli culture, a real legacy of God and Kings. Making him, to this day, the most read and questioned character in all humanity. But, how was the government that governed over the laws of Israel structured during Joseph and Mary's times? Why a NEW TESTAMENT? Like these, we could ask ourselves an endless number of questions about events related to Jesus.

Let's start by understanding what the Roman Empire meant and Joseph and Mary's social, political, and economic position.

The Roman emperor, Cesar Augustus, was the first Roman Emperor. He ruled between the years 27 B.C. and 14 A.D. making him the Roman Emperor with the longest reign in history.

In Israel, Herod the Great ruled as "King of the Jews." Israel was now a province belonging to the Roman Empire that would pay taxes to Rome. Herod was a tyrant and brutal man who made people obey him through fear and misery.

Joseph and Mary would have to live in Israel during challenging times. We know that Joseph's ancestors were of exceptional and distinguished lineage. Mary was not too far behind; she had among her ancestors Tamar, Ruth, Bathsheba, etc. All this would make them a highly accepted couple among the society of that time. Joseph was a carpenter and also a contractor, which placed him among those who lived well.

God analyzed all this before sending his son to earth as a human; he placed him in the womb of Mary, by the work and grace of the Holy Spirit, a virgin who was only committed to Joseph.

In those times, when a woman became pregnant under the same conditions as Mary's, Jewish society would condemn her to death. Therefore, it must have been tough for Joseph and Mary to face this situation. However, everything was part of God's plan; he had to keep Joseph and Mary in fear of God. He wanted them together to dedicate their lives to their son's care instead of being distracted by tribal life activities.

JESUS' BIRTH

Herod the Great, called "King of the Jews," was a Jew appointed King by Rome's senate because he was the perfect puppet that Rome needed in Judea. It was him who Jesus would have to face in his childhood and before he was born.

This is how Jesus the Messiah was born. His mother, Mary, was engaged to be married to Joseph. But before the marriage took place, while she was still a virgin, she became pregnant through the power of the Holy Spirit.

Joseph, to whom she was engaged, was a righteous man and did not want to disgrace her publicly, so he decided to break the engagement quietly. As he considered this, an angel of the Lord appeared to him in a dream. "Joseph, son of David," the angel said, "do not be afraid to take Mary as your wife. For the child within her was conceived by the Holy Spirit. And she will have a son, and you are to name him Jesus, for he will save his people from their sins."
(Matthew 1:18-21)

Let's take a closer look at God's wonderful plan for this family. The women of that time did not have a voice nor vote within the families that made up Hebrew society. They were considered only a patrimony of the father, who had to be bought. When Joseph got engaged to Mary, it was only because her father had agreed to it; Joseph made the acquisition of a virgin woman and became her owner. But Mary became pregnant without having sexual relations with him, making the agreement with his father-in-law a fraud. This crime was punishable by taking away the life of the woman via stoning.

There was a small detail. Joseph was not just any man, and

Mary was not just any woman. They both knew about God and the cultural heritage their ancestors had left them. Also, God knew of them and about the behavior of their ancestors. They understood each other, and God knew the heart of Joseph and his dynasty. That is why he sent an angel to give him the indication of his plan, knowing that he would carry it out.

After Jesus was born in Bethlehem in Judea, during the time of King Herod, Magi from the east came to Jerusalem and asked, "Where is the one who has been born king of the Jews? We saw his star when it rose and have come to worship him." King Herod was deeply disturbed when he heard this, as was everyone in Jerusalem.
(Matthew 2:1-3)

Herodes, as a Jew, knew of the prophecy that was told in Israel, of the house of David, and of the pact of God with David. After hearing that the prophecy had been fulfilled. Herod started imagining the loss of power and privileges, and with him, all those who accompanied him and those that made up his administration. Those who collected taxes and took property, those who exploited, humiliated, and served Cesar Augustus in Rome, who was the one to take the most. There was nothing he could do now to stop the prophecy. The most significant event in humanity had taken place. The son of God was born, the messiah, the Nazarene, the CHRIST, which means he was anointed by the LORD. And with it, a new time would begin to count and, to this day, the references before Christ (B.C.) and anno domini (A.D.), which in latin stands for "in the year of the lord," are still used.

THE NEW TESTAMENT is born. It would be written approximately seventy years after the death of Jesus; twenty-seven books written by the apostles and evangelists of the early church. It would take them seventy years to be recognized as books inspired by God and accepted as an expression of FAITH. But let's return to the subject of Jesus' birth,

After the wise men were gone, an angel of the Lord appeared to Joseph in a dream. "Get up! Flee to Egypt with the child and his mother," the angel said. "Stay there until I tell you to return, be-

**cause Herod is going to search for the child to kill him."
(Matthew 2:13)**

Herod did not know who the Son of God was, for the wise men did not return with him. Therefore, he gave the order to have all children under the age of two and born in Bethlehem killed. Herod, like countless rulers of different levels, gets sickened by the power. They lose their sense of responsibility to serve the people they govern and are capable of doing whatever it takes to remain in public office; they lie, steal, and kill. They undergo an exponential change of their personalities, and in the majority, not for good.

Herod would die, and his son Archelaus would rule in Judea, a man equal to or worse than his father. Judea was a region of Israel. When Joseph learned through an angel that this was happening in his country, he decided to leave Egypt for Galilee and live in Nazareth.

The Bible tells us that Jesus lived with his parents in Nazareth; hence they called him Nazarene. He lived in that region until the age of eleven or twelve, and, after leaving Nazareth, it would take twenty-some years for Jesus to reappear again. Where was he? There are many hypotheses. Wherever he was, no doubt he was preparing for the all-important assignment to fulfill his destiny.

JESUS' BAPTISM

Then Jesus went from Galilee to the Jordan River to be baptized by John. But John tried to talk him out of it. "I am the one who needs to be baptized by you," he said, "so why are you coming to me?" But Jesus said, "It should be done, for we must carry out all that God requires." So John agreed to baptize him. After his baptism, as Jesus came up out of the water, the heavens were opened and he saw the Spirit of God descending like a dove and settling on him. And a voice from heaven said, "This is my dearly loved Son, who brings me great joy."
(Matthew 3:13-17)

The mothers of John the Baptist and Mary, Jesus' mother, were cousins, so John and Jesus had a second-degree cousin relationship. The Bible says that John dressed in camel's skin or hair and ate honey and locusts. With this, he gives us an idea of the hermit life John lived in the desert, a life dedicated to meditation and communication with God, preparing to introduce his cousin, Jesus, before Israel society. But, what type of society did Israel have during the times of Jesus?.

We will say first that there was a procurator, also called a governor, and Rome appointed him. In the times of Jesus, Pontius Pilate was the procurator of Judea. At that time, Palestine was divided into regions called: Phoenician, Iturea, Galilee, Samaria, Judea, Perea, Idumea, and Decapolis. Eighth in total, each had its procurator or a representative under a procurator. All these regions had an obligation to pay two types of taxes to Rome:

DIRECT TAXES: They consisted of paying amounts of money in proportion to the number of properties they owned.

INDIRECT TAXES: they consisted of the percentages they

had to pay for the sales and purchases they made.

Pontious Pilate, as procurator of Judea in the time of Jesus, was responsible under the Roman Emperor's mandate to take full charge of the parcels, finances, the management of the supreme military power, and the collection of all taxes the Jews had to pay. He had the collectors under his command, backed by his soldiers, and also because the order to execute the death penalty was solely reserved for him.

The procurator was also responsible for appointing the high priest of Sanhedrin. The Sanhedrin was the supreme Jewish court, composed of the following social structures:

SADDUCEES.- It was the wealthiest and most influential Jewish social class that made up the Sanhedrin, preferred by the Roman Empire, so they were granted a tax collection monopoly. The SADDUCEES group was composed of the leading priestly families, including the High Priest, the great merchants, and the wealthiest landowners in the countryside. They were an aristocratic party that brought together the rich and powerful, few in number, but they were strongly organized in politics and justice administration.

They practiced religion, but they only accepted the TORAH, or the LAW OF MOSES, which includes the Pentateuch, made up of the first five books of the Bible; Genesis, Exodus, Leviticus, Numbers and Deuteronomy. They were fundamentalists of Judaism and rejected any other practice.

"Be careful," Jesus said to them. "Be on your guard against the yeast of the Pharisees and Sadducees."
(Matthew 16:6)

The high priest and his officials, who were Sadducees, were filled with jealousy.
(Acts 5:17)

Jesus said this to his followers because he knew how the Sadducees lived under loose traditions. They indulged in luxurious and pagan hobbies, following the example of the Romans. Divorce was frequent among them, thay used marriage between the same families to preserve power and wealth, and they could have as many women as they wanted, as long as they could support them.

The Sadducees were among those who persecuted the apostles and evangelists after the death of Jesus Christ. Believing in what Jesus preached implied losing their privileges, power and wealth. In general, they were of high social class and belonged to the aristocracy. Religiously, they were the main priests, and their influence was very powerful. Politically, they collaborated with the Romans to maintain their power.

THE HIGH PRIEST.- He was a Sadducee and the head of all Jews in Palestine and the foreigners. The High Priest was the main priest in charge of the temple. He was an administrator and the president of the Sanhedrin or great council. He was the only mortal who could enter the most intimate, sacred, and important part of the temple, "the Sancta Sanctorum," only three times in a day, one day of the year, such day was called "Day of Atonement" or "Yom Kippur" instituted by God.

MAIN PRIESTS.- The Temple's commander was responsible for
keeping order, three priests of the Treasury, and the Vigilant Priest kept the keys of the temple and was responsible for the vigilance and order under the authority of the Temple's Commander.

THE ELDERLY.- Also known as "Senators of the people," worked together with the high priests. Please note that in this case, they are not called The Elderly because they are old, but rather because they belonged to a group of the Sanhedrin composed only by the heads of the wealthiest and most powerful families amongst the Jews. They made up the aristocracy, the primary source of wealth for the temples, hence their relationship with the High Priests. They were linked to Roman power because the Romans gave them the concessions to collect taxes through the publicans. Because of this and the elderly, the Romans dominated the Sanhedrin. The fortunes of the elderly guaranteed the taxes imposed on the Jews would make it to the treasury of the Roman Empire intact, even though such taxes imposed by the Roman to the Jews far exceeded what they had to pay.

The Elders were only interested in establishing order and agreements because by doing so, they ensured the preservation and improvement of their economic, political and social position. For the elders, not doing their job well meant losing their privileges, being banished, and then having their property confiscated.

The Elders could not become priests, not even by buying the priesthood. They were only in charge of Rome's political and economic interests, their only idol was money, and they would kill if needed to obtain it.

The only Elder man the Bible mentions who followed a different course was the wealthy landowner Joseph of Arimathea. It was he who requested from Pontius Pilate the dead body of Jesus.

PHARISEES.- They were a religious group that distinguished itself for knowing well the Law of Moses. They made efforts to comply with the law and made others comply with it. They considered themselves the 'People of the Law'. Generally, they belonged to a low social class made up of artisans, small merchants, peasants. Even though their duty was to the people, the Pharisees kept their distance from the rest of the people because they seemed too ignorant of the law to socialize with them. They were considered hypocrites, since their livelihood and the activities they carried out depended on the same people they belittled. The Gospel that attacks the Pharisees the most is that of Matthew, which tell us:

They tie up heavy burdens, hard to bear, and lay them on people's shoulders, but they themselves are not willing to move them with their finger.
(Matthew 23:4)

SCRIBES.- They were "The specialists of the Law." Their power did neither come from money nor from inherited blood but from their knowledge. They were the Jewish intellectual aristocracy. The Pharisees-scribes came to the Sanhedrin with a solid understanding of the Old Testament. They perfectly mastered all the recesses of the Law, and they were appointed judges in the criminal and civil process. At the age of 40, scribes would receive the degree of "Graduate Doctor", which placed them in the most important positions of the education, administration, and justice systems. They had so much power that even the Pharisees' political party of the Sanhedrin was made up entirely of Scribes. Since the Sanhendrin was the only Supreme court of the Jews, they were the judges of almost all the important cities of Israel. The scribes were the ones who discussed the teachings of Christ, but only because they felt threatened, says the Bible:

When the leading priests and Pharisees heard this parable, they realized he was telling the story against them—they were the wicked farmers. They wanted to arrest him, but they were afraid of the crowds, who considered Jesus to be a prophet. (Matthew 21:45-46)

PUBLICANS.- They were the tax collectors, merchants who obtained from the state that rented their services the right to collect taxes. For this, they paid a certain amount of money to the government, keeping everything above what was agreed. There were two classes of tax collectors:

The Head of the Tax Collection System.- composed of the high society of the Sanhedrin, the Elderly. They were in charge of the exploitation and swindling of the Jews.

The Local Collectors.- The Publicans, made up mostly of slaves and the poor. A tax collection agency employed them.

The Publicans were despised by the Jews because they had to impose overpriced taxes to make a living. They were so poor and came from such a low society that even they accepted this dishonorable job to survive. Jesus' intervention with them was through Matthew, a Publican collector, also known as Levi.

Later, Levi held a banquet in his home with Jesus as the guest of honor. Many of Levi's fellow tax collectors and other guests also ate with them.
(Luke 5:29)

ZEALOTS.- This group, composed mainly of lower social classes, were considered troublemakers. They disagreed with the Romans and had an exaggerated zeal for Law enforcement. They encouraged frequent rebellions, which would be quelled quickly by the Roman forces. The zealots were the most radical wing of the Pharisees. They were fanatics who followed the first mandate that declared "Only God reigns in Israel." Known for being the most radical among nationalist Jews, they expressed themselves with terrorist acts directed against the Romans and other Jews who they considered to be less religious than them or any who opposed them. They especially despised the Jews who collaborated with the Romans.

ESSENES.- Their name means "Silent". They were men who lived in monastic-type communities under very austere and suffering lifestyles near the Dead Sea. They prayed and meditated on the scriptures awaiting the coming of the messiah. They were characters with a high sense of spirituality; hence they isolated themselves from other communities, and in isolation, they felt their approach to God.

It is believed that in the twenty-some years that Jesus is lost in the Gospels, he lived with them, preparing himself for the great task he had.

HELLENISTS.- They were the Jews born outside of Judea, mainly in North Africa and of the Eastern Mediterranean's shores near Greece or in Greece itself. They spoke Greek, hence the name Hellenes, they had their Synagogues, and they prayed in their language.

OTHER GROUPS.- Those who belonged to the lowest social

scale, the poor, the marginalized, those who nobody wanted to be close to because of the endless needs they suffered. Among them were "the farmers", who didn't even have enough land to make a living, the "hired workers" who worked only for food, "the artisans" consisted of bricklayers, blacksmiths, carpenters, etc. And the last group of people, those Jesus felt most inclined for, to the point of losing his life for them, consisted of women objectified by men, children, slaves, salaried shepherds, prostitutes, adulterers, beggars and the sick. The lack of food and hygiene in this marginalized society made people sick with leprosy, blindness, mental conditions, and nervous diseases unknown at the time; thus, those who had them were considered to be possessed.

The life of all these people was very harsh in general. The rich justified themselves by telling them they suffered only because they had sinned against God, and that was their punishment.

The Baptism of Jesus (Baptême de Jésus) by James Tissot Publication date 1886-1894 Topics art, European Art According to Matthew, Jesus travels from Galilee to Judaea to be baptized by John the Baptist in the Jordan River. Although John humbly protests and suggests that it is he who should be baptized by Jesus instead, Jesus insists. Here, a dove descends from the heavens as Jesus emerges from the water, while a voice from above calls him "my beloved Son."

JESUS' STRUCTURE

(THE APOSTLES)

Jesus, after noticing the structural conditions of the society of his time, opted to have his own structure, a fundamental principle in every visionary leader. He picked twelve men of different character and way of thinking, men who would continue to put aside their differences and ways of life.

Jesus called his twelve disciples together and gave them authority to cast out evil spirits and to heal every kind of disease and illness. Here are the names of the twelve apostles: first, Simon (also called Peter), then Andrew (Peter's brother), James (son of Zebedee), John (James's brother), Philip, Bartholomew, Thomas, Matthew (the tax collector), James (son of Alphaeus), Thaddaeus, Simon (the zealot), and Judas Iscariot (who later betrayed him). (Matthew 10:1-4)

But, who were these twelve men? And why did they choose to follow Jesus? Let's start with:

SIMON.- He is the apostle Simon Peter, the one who denied Jesus three times. **But Peter denied it again. A little later some of the other bystanders confronted Peter and said, "You must be one of them, because you are a Galilean."**
(Mark 14:70)

Peter was born in the Galilee Region, and he was a fisherman. Very little information is available about Peter before Jesus called him. The truth is those in the same line of work as Peter paid so much in taxes to the Romans, through the publicans, that it forced them into a precarious situation, which irritated Peter due to his strong character.

When Jesus called him, according to the Gospel of Matthew, he was made the leading apostle. Thus, he is mentioned as follows:

Now I say to you that you are Peter (which means 'rock'), and upon this rock I will build my church, and all the powers of hell will not conquer it. And I will give you the keys of the Kingdom of Heaven. Whatever you forbid on earth will be forbidden in heaven, and whatever you permit on earth will be permitted in heaven."
(Matthew 16:18-19)

Thereby, Peter was one of the most devoted defenders of Christianity.

After the death of Jesus, Peter presides over the replacement of Judas Iscariot after his death. It is Peter who speaks and addresses the crowd on the day of the Pentecost. He, who the Sanhedrin publicly examines along with John, is the first apostle to perform a public miracle: In the name of Jesus, he heals a man at the gates of the temple in Jerusalem. This is mentioned in the book of Acts, where Peter's figure stands out above the other apostles.

Peter's death occurred in Rome. Under Nero's command, he was martyred and crucified, but he asked to be crucified upside-down solely because he did not consider himself to be equal to Jesus Christ.

At the beginning of the 4th century, the emperor Constantine ordered St. Peter's Basilica's construction in Rome.

ANDREW.- Peter's brother, a fisherman too, was born in the town of Bethsaida in the Galilee region. He remained in chastity until marriage. Since he was of a lower class, he distanced himself entirely from the mundane things. When he heard that John the Baptist was preaching along the Jordan River banks, Andrew abandoned everything and left with him to become his disciple.

As Jesus walked by, John looked at him and declared, "Look! There is the Lamb of God!"
(John 1:36)

From that moment on, Andrew became the first follower of Jesus; hence he was considered the first Apostle of the Lord. He then looked for Peter and said: "We have found the Messiah." In general, the apostle Andrew had a very close relationship with Jesus during his public life; he was present in one of the miracles, as the one who said: "There's a little boy here who has five barley loaves and two fish. But that's a drop in the bucket for a crowd like this." He was present at the Last Supper, saw the risen Lord, witnessed the Lord's ascension, shared the graces and gifts of the first Pentecost, and helped, despite threats of persecution, to establish FAITH in Palestine.

He died in Patrae of Achaia in Greece. He asked to be crucified in a different way than Jesus, so he was martyred and crucified on an X-shaped cross. During the last three days of his life on the cross, through the agony, he preached to those who approached. That cross is now commonly known as "Saint Andrew's Cross."

JAMES, SON OF ZEBEDEE.- James, son of Zebedee and Salome, a fisherman and high-humble status like his brother John. He was usually with Jesus. James witnessed the resurrection of Jairus' daughter **(Mark 5:35-42)**, the transfiguration at Mount Tabor **(Luke 9:28-29)**, the prayer in the Olive gardens with Simon, Peter and his brother John. He also witnessed the last appearance of the risen Lord on the shores of Lake Tiberias (Sea of Galilee) and the miraculous fishing **(John 21:1-8)**

He was killed by the sword in A.D. 43 by orders of the king of Judea, Herod Agrippa I. He was apprehended while he was preaching and then martyred in Jerusalem prior to his death. He was one of the first Christians martyred and persecuted by King Herod. After noticing such acts pleased the wealthy classes of Sanhedrin, all Jews, also ordered Peter to be arrested in order to generate alliances between them.

JOHN.- Son of Zebedee and Salome, brother of James. It is believed that these two apostles, despite not being wealthy, were the ones with the highest economic and social status among the apostles because Zebedee, his father, and brothers were the owners of the fishing business, the nets, and the boats, and had paid workers. It is likely that due to the social and economic status of Zebedee, they had commercial connections in Jerusalem and even maintained a good relationship with the Temple. It could be said that Jesus, John, and James were first cousins, since John and James' mother was Mary's sister, mother of Jesus. John is considered the youngest apostle of Jesus and one of the most outstanding disciples. Jesus called him and James "Sons of Thunder" for their great impetus.

John spent most of his time with Jesus. He was also present in miracles, witness the resurrection of Jairus' daughter, the transfiguration of Jesus in the Garden of Gethsemane where Jesus retired to pray after the coming of his passion and his death, and was present in the appearance of the risen Jesus and the miraculous fishing in the Sea of Tiberias.

Many authors consider John as the beloved disciple of Jesus because, at the Last Supper, he is the one who rests on his chest. It is estimated that due to the socio-economic position that John had, he could associate himself with the Sanhedrin. **Simon Peter followed Jesus, as did another of the disciples. That other disciple was acquainted with the high priest, so he was allowed to enter the high priest's courtyard with Jesus. Peter had to stay outside the gate. Then the disciple who knew the high priest spoke to the woman watching at the gate, and she let Peter in.** (John 18:15-16)

Through these biblical passages, we learn that John is Jesus' cousin and that they had an excellent close relationship with each other. John is the apostle in charge of the intermediation between Jesus and the aristocratic classes. Only those who had money could talk to the High Priest, and it was evident that John had money, a high social position, and culture for such things.

John died of old age at approximately 98 years old in the ancient city of Ephesus, Turkey, according to some authors; others say that on the Island of Patmos, Greece. But, what matters most is that he left us a great legacy of wisdom in his Gospel, the Epistles, and the Revelation. These books make up the New Testament.

PHILIP.- He was born in the city of Bethsaida, the same town where Peter and Andrew were born. He was a Galilean and a fisherman, a low class and a follower of John the Baptist. He was the fifth apostle called by Jesus. Philip participated in three crucial episodes:

Jesus soon saw a huge crowd of people coming to look for him. Turning to Philip, he asked, "Where can we buy bread to feed all these people?" He was testing Philip, for he already knew what he was going to do. Philip replied, "Even if we worked for months, we wouldn't have enough money to feed them!" (John 6:5-7)

With this biblical passage, we understand that Philip was an ordinary person of that time. His answer places him as a salaried worker; therefore, he knew of the famine conditions those in low-class society lived under.

Now among those who went up to worship at the feast were some Greeks. They came to Philip, who was from Bethsaida in Galilee, with a request. "Sir," they said, "we would like to see Jesus." Philip told Andrew about it, and they went together to ask Jesus.
(John 12:20-22)

On this other, Philip shows a lack of leadership and initiative as the leading follower of Jesus.

Philip said to him, "Lord, show us the Father, and it is enough for us."Jesus replied, "Have I been with you all this time, Philip, and yet you still don't know who I am? Anyone who has seen me has seen the Father! So why are you asking me to show him to you?
(John 14:8-9)

And lastly, through these passages, Philip shows a lack of Faith regarding the trinity that dwells in Jesus.

These three events give us a general idea of Philip's personality, a naive and innocent man, somewhat timid and with a judicious mind.

Philip died in Hierapolis, where he preached, he was martyred and crucified upside-down and then stoned to death. He died somewhat old but left a great legacy of Christianity in Asia Minor, present-day Turkey.

BARTHOLOMEW.- He was born in Cana in the Galilee region. He was introduced to Jesus through Philip. Bartholomew is mentioned in various biblical passages of the four Gospels and Acts.

Later, Jesus appeared again to the disciples beside the Sea of Galilee. This is how it happened. Several of the disciples were there—Simon Peter, Thomas (nicknamed the Twin), Nathanael (Bartholomew) from Cana in Galilee, the sons of Zebedee, and two other disciples.
(John 21:1-2)

In the Gospel of Matthew, he is mentioned as one of the twelve. **(Matthew 10:1-4)**

In the Gospel of Mark, he is also mentioned as one of the twelve. **(Mark 3: 14-19)**

In Luke, as one of the twelve. **(Luke 6:13-16)**

In the book of Acts, he is mentioned as a council member to replace Judas Iscariot, who had died, with Matthew, who in luck won over Joseph, also known as Barsabas. **(Acts 1:12-26)**

Bartholomew left Asia Minor to accompany Philip to India, where he died because of his preaching. He was martyred by being skinned alive at the edge of the knife and then beheaded.

THOMAS.- Little is known about this apostle's life before joining Jesus. We know that he was Galilean and a fisherman.

His most famous intervention in Christianity is his disbelief about the resurrection of Jesus. Here is how it happened:

Now Thomas, one of the twelve called the Twin, was not with them when Jesus came. They told him, "We have seen the Lord!" But he replied, "I won't believe it unless I see the nail

wounds in his hands, put my fingers into them, and place my hand into the wound in his side."

Eight days later the disciples were together again, and this time Thomas was with them. The doors were locked; but suddenly, as before, Jesus was standing among them.

"Peace be with you!" he said.

Then he said to Thomas, "Put your finger here, and look at my hands. Put your hand into the wound in my side. Don't be faithless any longer. Believe!"

Thomas answered him, "My Lord and my God!"

Then Jesus told him, "You believe because you have seen me. Blessed are those who believe without seeing me." (John 20:24-29)

Everything indicates that Thomas was pessimistic, he did not doubt his love for Jesus, and he felt very sorry for the passion and death of the Lord. Perhaps, since he wanted to assimilate the death of Jesus alone, he had separated a little from the group, so when they told him that Jesus had appeared, the news seemed too beautiful to believe it was true. However, Thomas had another virtue: When he was convinced of his beliefs, he followed them through to the end, with all of their consequences. We owe him the beautiful profession of FAITH, "My Lord and my God," for that reason he went to spread the gospel until he died martyred for proclaiming his FAITH in the risen Jesus Christ in India. It must have been quite an incredible disbelief from Thomas for Jesus to say: "Blessed are those who believe without seeing me."

MATTHEW.- He was born in Capernaum and collected taxes before following Jesus. Without a doubt, Matthew was out of the twelve apostles, the one who best knew the social, economic, and political conditions of his time. His occupation was much hated by the Jews because he collected money from them to another nation. Matthew was a publican who, at the time that Jesus called him, earned very little from the collection since most of it was taken by the Sanhedrin, who were the ones to grant the publicans the right to collect, the Sadducees administered this activity with permission from the governor or procurator in the service of Rome.

Matthew is mentioned in the four Gospels of Christianity repeatedly. We owe the Gospel of Matthew to Matthew himself. It contains only twenty-eight chapters and has been a delight for preachers of the Word of Jesus for twenty centuries in all continents. He died in Hierapolis, Turkey, martyred.

JAMES, SON OF ALPHEUS.- Jacob was Jesus' first cousin, given that his father Alpheus, also known as Cleophas, was the brother of Joseph of Nazareth, father of Jesus and husband of Mary. He was born in Cana of Galilee and was present in most events, miracles, and the resurrection of Jesus. It is essential to know that this James is often identified as James "The minor" because of his small stature. He was one of the leaders of the church in Jerusalem, but for fear of rejection by the Jews, he ended up Judaizing Christianity, making followers of Christian doctrine turn to Jew doctrine. The apostle Paul repeatedly criticized him for his actions. James eventually understood that God had offered salvation through grace to the Gentiles, seeing that there was no difference between both groups; they both could compose a single body through the church.

James is the clear example of how we can fall into doctrinal error and rectify it through the Holy Spirit. James was called "Divine Seed" because he cultivated the seed of the Word of God in the hearts of men; he planted FAITH and cultivated PIETY. He died in Jerusalem as an older man, approximately in the year 62 A.D.

THADDAEUS.- Known as Judas Thaddaeus, son of Cleophas or Alphaeus, he descended from David's royal line. He was Jesus' first cousin and the brother of the apostle James "The Minor." The relationship with Jesus is that Joseph and Alphaeus were brothers, parents of both.

Thaddaeus accompanied Jesus on his pilgrimage and miracles, he is credited with one of the epistles that were not addressed to any person, community, or church but rather encouraged Christians to fight courageously to defend the FAITH and Christianity doctrine. Thaddaeus is distinguished by the fact that after the last supper he asked Jesus:

But, Lord, why do you intend to show yourself to us and not to the world?

Jesus replied, "All who love me will do what I say. My Father will love them, and we will come and make our home with each of them."

(John 14:22-23)

With this, Thaddaeus shows that he has excellent sensitivity and the gift of service because the question he asks Jesus is looking for the common good in general. Nevertheless, it must be Jesus himself who clarifies he lives within those who fulfill what he says.

Judas Thaddaeus was born in Cana of Galilee and was also of humble origin. He died in Persia defending his Christian FAITH at the hands of pagan leaders who worshiped idols and repudiated the preaching of the apostles Judas Thaddaeus and Simon; both were sacrificed and martyred. Simon was cut in half with a saw, and Thaddaeus' head was cut off with an ax in 70 A.D.

SIMON, THE ZEALOT.- He was considered the guerilla fighter, of low class, with an exaggerated zeal for law enforcement. Before following Christ, he fought against Rome. He was born in Cana of Galilea.

This apostle may have followed Jesus for political reasons. When Jesus was arrested in the Garden of Gethsemane, among the apostles, there were two swords, one wielded by Peter, who was the one that cut off the ear of the Sanhedrin's servant, and the other one wielded by a weapons expert, Simon, The Zealot. Why did Simon not draw his sword then? The most prudent would be to think that, when he initially started to follow Jesus, his intentions were purely political, but over time he began to understand the teachings of the Lord, he understood that the way to achieve freedom is not by the sword, but by following Jesus with unquestionable loyalty.

It is true that the Zealots, Simon's sect, were the first to create an opposition party against the Roman Empire. The party was drawn by a religious sense that wanted to combat Roman Paganism and defend Jewish Law.

The Zealots were wrong about Jesus Christ since they knew of his lineage with David, they believed Jesus would start an armed revolution in Israel. Thus they had long awaited the arrival of a liberator who would continue down the same path as those great prophets of Israel.

The day the apostle Simon fully met Jesus, when he sincerely converted to the gospel and began to follow him, he witnessed the wonders that Jesus performed, falling completely in love with the Christian Gospel. Thus this was the reason why he was killed in Persia, on the shores of the Black Sea, together with his companion the apostle Thaddeus.

JUDAS ISCARIOT.- Very little is known of Judas Iscariot before Jesus called him. It is believed that he was born in a town in Judea and that, like Simon, the Zealot, he joined the Christian cause, more for political than religious purposes. In the Gospel of John, they mention him like this, when Mary washes Jesus' feet with expensive perfume he says: **"That perfume was worth a year's wages. It should have been sold and the money given to the poor." He said this, not because he cared about the poor, but because he was a thief; as keeper of the money bag, he used to help himself to what was put into it.**
(John 12:5-6)

With this we realize the internal differences that existed between the apostles and Judas Iscariot.

The gospels say that he followed Jesus during his preaching in Palestine, but they point him out as the traitor who told the Sanhedrin who Jesus and his followers were. He led these Jewish representatives of the power of that time to Jesus, and he signaled who Jesus was with a kiss on the cheek. For that act, Judas collected thirty silver coins, a small capital he, repentant of what he had done, tried to return, but those who had given the coins did not want to take them back. He threw them inside the temple and then proceeded to hang himself from a tree.

MATTHIAS.- He is the one who replaced Judas Iscariot after his death. This was the only occasion in which the apostles decided to replace someone who had caused casualties. Matthias was made an apostle because he had earned the trust of Christianity by being a loyal follower of Jesus, from the moment that John the Baptist baptized Jesus until the time of his death.

In the book of Acts, it is mentioned that it was by luck that he won such a distinction out of the two candidates with sufficient merits to occupy that position. The other one was Joseph, also known as Barsabas.

The apostle Matthias was born in Bethlehem of Judah. In a very noble family, he was very educated in the law and very intelligent. He was always careful to practice what he preached to others.

Through the wonders and miracles that God allowed him to do, he converted many into Christians in Judea. This provoked hatred among the Jews, who sentenced him to die stoned and decapitated with an ax once dead. That is how the Apostle Matthias died.

The Last Supper: Judas Dipping his Hand in the Dish
by James Tissot

Publication date 1886-1894 Topics art, European Art

For the Passover feast, the apostles (dressed in traveling clothes, like the Jews of the Old Testament book of Exodus, Tissot explains) meet in a room decorated with garlands. During the meal, Jesus reveals that he will be betrayed by one of his disciples; many of them worriedly ask, "Is it I?"

In this image, Jesus hands the sop, or dipped bread, to Judas Iscariot, identifying him as the traitor. Jesus later dismisses him from the company, urging him to be quick about his business.

Here, John the Evangelist, described as the "beloved disciple," lays his head on Jesus' shoulder, as is traditional in scenes of the Last Supper. By contrast, Judas, across the table, is already distanced from Jesus, spatially as well as spiritually. And while all the rest of the company wears white, Judas' robes are dark.

JESUS IN A POSITION OF WAR

Jesus knew that the Roman Empire, which ruled over Israel at the time he preached, was the most powerful in the known world. They ruled by sowing fear, misery, despair and abandonment. Jesus had Jewish allies who helped him subdue other Jews; they were brothers of race, creed, ideology, and culture. The townspeople saw Jesus as a salvation alternative because of his royal lineage. They believed he could liberate Palestine. However, what could he do in a situation like this?

Jesus knew very well that the Roman Empire had social structures, weapons, horses, and money and could acquire any defense system if threatened. Anyone who rose against it was ruthlessly crushed to serve as an example to others.

Jesus knew that nothing was going to be accomplished by raising arms and that by doing so, he would only condemn his followers to appalling deaths and martyrdom.

His plan was God's plan, and he focused his doctrine on those who could hear and accept him, who had nothing or almost nothing to lose. He chose the poorest, the lowest, and most needy social classes in Palestine.

Jesus addressed the upper classes at the time, mainly Jews who made up the Sanhedrin and those who served them, to make a declaration of war, he told them :

"No one can serve two masters. For you will hate one and love the other; you will be devoted to one and despise the other. You cannot serve God and be enslaved to money.

(Matthew 6:24)

"Don't store up treasures here on earth, where moths eat them and rust destroys them, and where thieves break in and steal. Store your treasures in heaven, where moths and rust cannot destroy, and thieves do not break in and steal. Wherever your treasure is, there the desires of your heart will also be.
(Matthew 6:19-21)

…Jesus looked around and said to his disciples, "How hard it is for the rich to enter the Kingdom of God!"
(Mark 10:17-23)

But the worries of this life, the deceitfulness of wealth and the desires for other things come in and choke the word, making it unfruitful.
(Mark 4:19)

And he said to them, "You have a fine way of rejecting the commandment of God in order to establish your tradition!"
(Mark 7:9)

Then he said, "Beware! Guard against every kind of greed. Life is not measured by how much you own."
(Luke 12: 15)

"What sorrow awaits you who are rich, for you have your only happiness now."
(Luke 6:24)

… "But Abraham said to him, 'Son, remember that during your lifetime you had everything you wanted, and Lazarus had nothing. So now he is here being comforted, and you are in anguish…'"(Luke 16:19-31)

Here's the lesson: Use your worldly resources to benefit others and make friends. Then, when your possessions are gone, they will welcome you to an eternal home.
(Luke 16:9)

Then the Lord said to him, "You Pharisees are so careful to clean the outside of the cup and the dish, but inside you are filthy —full of greed and wickedness!"
(Luke 11:39)

For as the body apart from the spirit is dead, so also faith apart from works is dead.
(James 2:26)

For the love of money is the root of all kinds of evil. And some people, craving money, have wandered from the true faith and pierced themselves with many sorrows.

(1 Timothy 6:10)

THE JEWISH WOMAN

In the times of Jesus, the status of women in Jewish society was shameful. The father ruled Jewsih families, and he did so as an absolute lord. He owned the family's assets, and their heirs could only be men. The daughters, on the other hand, only increased the family assets. If a suitor wanted to buy them, they had to be virgins, and if the man happened to say that she was not a virgin after marriage with him, death would await her in a lapidary manner. The father of the family was the one who gave orders, punished, pronounced the prayers, offered sacrifices, and educated the children. The mother was considered inferior to the man because she had very few advantages over him. She was only respected and revered by the children she had because they were gifts and blessings from God. The father could not arrange marriage for any of his daughters younger than 13 years old. Men had to wait for women to grow up until they could acknowledge the man they wanted to marry, but the man had to have money to buy her; otherwise, the father would not allow it even if she wanted to. If the father consented to the relationship and the daughters married, the husband would become the woman's owner, and she could not keep any of the income from her work or any she could find.

In general, the woman belonged entirely to her owner. If she was single, she belonged to the father; if married, she belonged to the husband; and if she was a childless widow, she belonged to her brother-in-law. Women were kept in extreme poverty to subdue them quickly. In the Gospel of Mark **(12:41-43)**, Jesus noticed a widow placing two coins of little value in the offerings, and he also saw others depositing large sums. Jesus called his disciples and made it clear to them that the widow had given all her wealth and, instead, the others had given only their pocket change. In these passages, we realize that Jesus perfectly knew the Palestine woman's condition, a condition that outraged him, as seen in many other biblical passages.

THE JEWISH REACTION AGAINST JESUS

In the time of Jesus, it was expected the rich and powerful Jews would feel offended and aggravated with the preachings and testimonies of the miracles of Jesus. They saw that many people followed him and feared their interests of wealth and power were at stake. Let's take a look at some biblical passages to notice the Jewish participation of those who composed the Sanhedrin in the crucifixion and death of Jesus Christ.

The leading priests and teachers of religious law were plotting how to kill Jesus, but they were afraid of the people's reaction.
(Luke 22:2)

So the Jewish leaders began harassing Jesus for breaking the Sabbath rules.
(John 5:16)

After that, he taught daily in the Temple, but the leading priests, the teachers of religious law, and the other leaders of the people began planning how to kill him. But they could think of nothing, because all the people hung on every word he said.
(Luke 19:47-48)

At that same time the leading priests and elders were meeting at the residence of Caiaphas, the high priest, plotting how to capture Jesus secretly and kill him.
(Matthew 26:3-4)

Among others, these biblical passages expose that the high social class of the Jews were the most interested in the death of Jesus Christ. And to accomplish such an act, they had to agree with each other and then with the government because only the government could sentence the death penalty since, in the Jewish law of the Sanhedrin, they did not possess the power to apply the death penalty.

Judas Iscariot would be the one to lead the Sanhedrin to arrest Jesus, pointing him out with a kiss on the cheek. Already in their hands, they thought that, if Rome executed him, the romans would take the blame, so they chose to hand him over to Pontious Pilate, procurator of Judea. They accused Jesus of lying about Moses' Law and of rebellion against Rome, and they wanted to make the procurator believe that Jesus was a revolutionary who endangered the Roman Empire. A grave error because Pontious Pilate was a "politician" who only allowed himself to be deceived when it was convenient for him, he was well aware that Jesus was from Galilee. A region where Herod ruled, so he sent Jesus for Herod to deal with him. However, Herod was just another politician who also feared the Jews would turn against him if he dealt with the death of Jesus; thus, he thought it would be best to return him to Pontious Pilate. However he did not want problems in his town, his "little goose that laid golden eggs," therefore he gave them a choice between Barabbas, a prisoner accused of rioting and murder in the city of Jerusalem, and Jesus.

The plan of the Sanhedrin was the death of Jesus, who had already been sentenced. They chose Barabbas to be released and, with this, Pontious Pilate had washed his hands in a symbolic act of his innocence and proceeded with the sentence for the will of the Sanhedrin was to be carried out, so he crucified him.

After this, it was a matter of time for the Christian effervescence to diminish and for the Jewish Aristocrats to continue in the same economic, political, and social positions they had.

It would be the apostles, preachers, and followers of Jesus who spread Christianity to this day. On one hand, some are trying to create awareness in love for GOD and the NEIGHBOR. On the other hand, others are defending interests of money and power, for the simple reason that every one of us within ourselves has sown the seeds of good and evil. It is up to each of us to instill the conscience that brings equilibrium to the life we want to live and the one we expect after our flesh dies.

This book's nature is solely educational so that the intention of good relationships between governments and the governed is spread among our society in general so that we can elect people fearful of GOD. This way, the former governor can exercise his power well and the successor, in the form of a PACT, be an observer and propagator of the same acceptable practices of the government, whether at the city, state, or federal level, and that by walking together we make our society a conviviality of mutual respect and peace, a culture in which granting public power to men and women is an act of maturity and responsibility, where rulers and ruled give their best, and are role models among their families, friends and the general public.

Thanks for Reading!
Leave a review on Amazon and let me know what you thought.

THE END

ABOUT THE AUTHOR

Oscar Pulido Fuentes

I am a man who walks in the light of God, one who seeks to do well by others via honesty and integrity. I have a beautiful family who means the world to me; my wife and partner ever since I had just graduated from college, and my two sons, who also recently graduated college, are my pride and joy. I have dedicated most of my adult life to public and social service and currently am a militant of a movement that battles the current ways the government is used to be run in Mexico. We want to go back to the years when the government served and worked for its people and not the other way around. I believe the world is constantly changing to adapt to current events and present times, sometimes for good but others for bad. And it is up to us to do something about it and not be complacent about what happens around us, but instead, act upon what can be done to change that what is not working or no longer works in the way it is intended to. Me writing this book is one of those actions I intend to take to inspire and spread awareness among those who seek it and those who may require it.

ACKNOWLEDGEMENT

"I have to start by thanking my awesome wife, Juany for reading early drafts and my two sons Oscar and Oziel for giving me advice on the cover, editing and translating this book. They were as important to this book getting done as I was. Thank you all"